THE MAN WHO
PLUNDERED THE CITY

The Man Who Plundered the City

Sven Elvestad

Translated by FREDERICK H. MARTENS

ROBERT M. McBRIDE & COMPANY
NEW YORK   1924

CONTENTS

CHAPTER I

THE ROBBER OF THE VILLA ROSENHAIN

"I 'll go as far as to say," remarked the Chief of Police, as he laid down some papers which he had just read very carefully, "that my men have done all that was humanly possible in this matter. Yet they only have wasted their time. Today we are just where we were four weeks ago, and have not made a single step ahead in solving the mystery. It stands to reason that the public is beginning to show signs of nervousness. And the worst of it is that general attention has been called to the strange and mysterious nature of this series of crimes. If there is another robbery like that of the ship-chandler, Vogt, the public will be seriously alarmed. And in that case the police will be to blame, as usual!"

"Don't get the idea in your head that I am afraid of the newspapers, or the steps public opinion may take in that case. I know that the police have done everything that possibly could be done. But you can realize that too great an interest on the part of the public may easily interfere with the course of our investigations. For that reason it is not alone desirable, but it is absolutely essential for us to get results of some kind. At any rate, we must prevent any repetition of these crimes, for they would be sure to cause excitement. And since I want to leave no stone unturned, and do not wish to have anything 'thrown up' to me later on, I have decided, after consulting my most trustworthy lieutenants, to ask the aid of a man whose ability is recognized by the majority of the public, and whose bulldog tenacity and intelligence I am the first to acknowledge."

Such were the wellweighed words spoken by the Chief of Police in his office on the afternoon of August 23rd, 1909, and the person to whom he was speaking, private detective Asbjörn Krag, sat listening to him with a discouraged air, without saying a word, and sucking a black cigar.

Arranging the papers on his desk, the Chief of Police went on:

"As I have already told you," he said, "we have a few, a very few clues."

At these words Krag raised his eyes, but they did not meet those of the Chief, for the latter was bending over his papers.

"It must be said," murmured the tall, thin, serious official, "that we do handle things pretty well in Christiania now. Even in New York or in London a series of mysterious crimes like those on record here would attract attention. No doubt you have seen what little has been published in the papers about what has happened?"

"For a long time I have suspected that these crimes, in spite of the differences between them, all can be traced back to the same source. They all point to one and the same master mind. And now the newspapers are beginning to hint the same thing— and that means a scandal! Or, to be more exact, it means a 'sensational disclosure,' one of those infernal sensations which so often have held us back in our work. We must take care that nothing of the kind happens."

The Chief of Police stopped for a moment, and then went on:

"The whole thing began when the home of Stefanson, the bank president, the Villa Rosenhain, was entered on July 23rd, at ten o'clock, P. M."

"Ten-thirty, P. M.," murmured detective Krag. It was the first word he had spoken for some time. The Chief looked a bit surprised, glanced at his reports again, then nodded:

"Right," said he. "You will remember that the president was giving an anniversary party, and while the party was going on, his wife's jewels were stolen. They were worth ten thousand crowns. There was no clue to show how the robber had entered the house, and the jewel-case had been opened quietly by an experienced hand."

"I remember. The jewel-case was in Mrs. Stefanson's room, and the doors to the rooms adjoining were locked. The guests were near at hand, but no one heard a sound. Mrs. Stefanson's room was on the first floor, but all the windows were found locked from the inside. All this I know."

"Very well. But do you know that not *one* of the stolen jewels ever has been recovered? As a rule, in the case of such robberies, we can find a clue in our own pawn-brokers' shops, or in those abroad. But these jewels disappeared without leaving a single trace. We have investigated in Christiania, New York, London, Paris, Berlin—but not the very smallest pearl of Mrs. Stefanson's handsome collection ever has turned up. What do you think of such a robbery?"

"The robber must have been some one who was staying inside the house at the time."

The Chief of Police slapped his reports down on the desk impatiently:

"The servants, yes, the servants," he murmured. "But we could not find a single suspect among them."

"Among the servants?" murmured Krag and once more raised his eyes.

"I know what you mean," growled the Chief, angrily. "Of course a detective can suspect any one and every one. But don't ask me to suspect the ladies and gentlemen who were Stefanson's guests that night. One and all, they belong to Christiania's upper circles. They included the cashier of his bank, and members of the bank's board of directors, Stefanson's personal friends, all of them socially prominent. So far as I know all of them are very wealthy men, and it is simply ridiculous to imagine that they could have been guilty of this wretched jewel robbery. Besides, you must not forget the next robberies. Three days later several valuable contracts were taken from the ship Chandler Björneby's private safe. The safe had been opened in the same clever way. Then, a week later, the safe of Wold, the retired financier, was plundered in the same fashion, while he was entertaining company. And the thieves got away with twenty thousand crowns in gold and notes. The old miser had no faith in banks, and always kept large sums of money in the house. Of course we investigated every one of his guests, and it turned out that not one of them had been a guest at Stefanson's affair. You saw the advertisement in the paper?"

"I did."

"Wold had noted down the numbers of five one-thousand crown notes that were lying with the gold. We have published the numbers of these notes in practically every paper in Norway, Sweden and Denmark. We have sent a warning to every exchange bank abroad, yet we have received no report of any attempt to pass one of these bank-notes. You must admit that it is enough to drive one mad. And now we come to the pockets picked in the National Theatre at the special performance on August 5th. Five gentlemen in the orchestra were robbed of their bill-folds, and even the king's guest, Prince Chira, of Siam, who was present, lost his grand cross of the Order of St. Vladimir, set in diamonds, and a very valuable stick-pin, in the foyer of the building. This does not seem to have anything to do with the safes which were robbed and broken open, yet I suspect that the same shrewd criminal was at the bottom of it. He seems to be a fellow who prefers to operate in places where some sort of festivity, with music and dancing, is going on. And he must be a robber who is bored to death with burglary along old-fashioned lines. For one cannot help thinking that it must be much harder to do 'professional' work of the kind when there are many people present, than in the silence of the night, when it is dark and every one is asleep. But now we reach the last case, the strangest one of all."

"You mean the daring robbery at No. 54 Pine Street?" asked Krag.

The Chief of Police nodded, and drew from his bundle of reports a small scrap of paper on which were written a few type-written lines.

"You will see," he said to Krag, as he handed him the scrap of paper, "what a daring criminal the fellow is."

Krag took the paper and read the mysterious message it contained:

"If you wish to find the thief of the Villa Rosenhain, you must pay attention to the revolver-shot which will go off tonight, at eleven thirty-seven in No. 54 Pine Street."

The Chief of Police pressed an electric button.

"And now," said he, "we will have in the man who heard the shot and saw what happened."

A newcomer entered the office. He was a muscular man of about thirty-five, with a red-cheeked, good-natured, smiling face. But the eyes in this good-natured face were uncommonly quick and watchful. Krag at once recognized him and gave him a friendly word of greeting. It was Police Inspector Helgesen. He had come to the big city as a farmer boy, and entering the police force, had proved himself so clever and able that he had been rapidly advanced, and now held a position of confidence.

"Well, you gentlemen are old acquaintances," growled the Chief of Police, "so no introductions are necessary. You probably know what it is all about, Helgesen. It is the Stefanson business!"

Turning to Krag, he went on:

"We have checked up the crimes which were committed after the first house-breaking in Stefanson's Villa Rosenhain. Tell us, Helgesen, what happened the other night in No. 54 Pine Street."

Helgesen sat down at the table, and as soon as he saw that Krag was to be drawn into the game, became interested.

"Yes," said he, "if you can find an answer to that riddle, you are a very clever man, for it is about the most complicated and difficult case with which I ever have had anything to do. First I'll tell you about No. 54 Pine Street, and later about the attempt made in the picture-gallery, which is also interesting because, owing to a strange combination of circumstances, the thief was foiled.

"As soon as we received the mysterious letter," Helgesen continued, "we did not lose a moment finding out who lived at No. 54. It was a one-family house, the property of the immensely wealthy Captain Karstens, who married a daughter of Rydberg, the bank president—you know who I mean. I sent men out into the neighborhood to pick up what information they could, got in touch with the servants, etc., and in a couple of hours' time we knew that, to summarize briefly:

"1. Captain Karstens lived at home.

"2. He was giving a party on August 7th.

"3. He was expecting fifty guests.

"4. He was looking for good extra help to wait on these guests.

"5. Among the guests the Ambassador from Mexico was the only foreigner. All the others invited were Norwegians, mostly from Christiania, and mostly officers, though there were also a couple of university professors and one artist, the well-known comedian Trybel. There is the list, Krag. The invitations already had been sent out. You probably will recognize most of the names."

Krag took up the paper which Helgesen handed him and studied it carefully. Then, handing it back to the Inspector, he said:

"I know all the names."

"Good," replied Helgesen. "And now, which of these ladies or gentlemen would you suspect of the theft of two thousand crowns from the locked drawer of a writing-desk, in addition to the robbery of five thousand crowns' worth of jewels from the jewel-case belonging to the lady of the house?"

Krag smiled.

"I would not suspect a single one—or, I would suspect them all. But who fired the shot?"

Helgesen nodded.

"Then you know about the shot which was fired? That was the queerest thing of all. When I had found out what I have just shown you, I made up my mind to be in the house on the night of the party.

The Captain, as I have said, was looking for extra help. I reported and was taken on. As you know, a good criminal inspector must be a good waiter, too. It is seldom that one gets a better chance to 'size up' a situation than when walking around with a napkin over one's arm. At eight-thirty the guests began to arrive, and at nine dinner was served in the big dining-room. Let me call your attention to the fact that the house is two-storied, with a mansard roof. The big dining-hall is built in duplex style, and runs from the second story to the roof. It is lighted from the side, and from above and, including the mansard, may be said to occupy two stories. The smoking-room and drawing-rooms, by the way, are situated in the southern wing of the second story. A broad flight of stairs leads down into the hall, which is the central point from which branches out a suite of big, handsome rooms. The Captain's house is a very fine villa. It is a well-known and prominent house in an elegant neighborhood. In fact, you might almost call it a palace.

"Well, the dinner ran its usual course without my noticing the least thing out of the way. I had a chance to study every one of the guests—most of whom I knew by appearance—and had to smile at the idea that the criminal we were in search of might be among them. Toward eleven o'clock the company rose from the table in a very jolly mood, especially some of the older officers who had done full justice to Captain Karstens' first-class wine-cellar.

"The numerous guests dispersed through the house, though most of them gathered in the big smoking-room where the comedian Trybel was preparing to entertain them with a couple of his best numbers. But there were groups of people talking and laughing in nearly all the other rooms, excepting, of course, the Karstens' private suite. And by this time the guests were all on such an easy footing with each other that if a stranger suddenly had appeared (such a thing might have happened), he would at once have attracted attention.

"But I know what is in your mind now, my dear Krag. You are thinking of the rest of the hired help. Quite right. And I do not mind telling you that I had made it my business to find out exactly who they were. There were four others, five including myself, and I was pretty certain of their whereabouts almost every minute of the time. I also kept an eye on the Captain's regular staff of servants; and as for the men in the garage, they were entertaining a visitor known to one of them who was one of my detectives. So it is not too much to say that every one was watched. Time went on, and it got to be eleven-thirty. I had almost begun to think that nothing would happen, and that our anonymous note had only been written to have a laugh at the expense of

the police. But that very moment I accidentally noticed Captain Karstens and his wife talking together
in a low tone of voice. They had met by the great
stair column in the hall, and since I could see by the
Captain's face that something had happened, I carefully edged my way close enough to them to be able
to catch their whispers.

" 'It must have happened during dinner,' I heard
Captain Karstens say.

" 'Do you think so?' answered his wife.

" 'Yes,' said he. 'I am sure it did, for I put the
portfolio in my writing-desk when I started to dress
for dinner.'

" 'And did you lock the desk?'

" 'Yes, and now it is broken open.'

"When I heard Captain Karstens say this my
ears, naturally, began to stretch a little further in his
direction, and I listened with the keenest interest to
the remainder of the conversation.

" 'How much money was there in it?' asked Mrs.
Karstens.

" 'Two thousand crowns, more or less,' said the
Captain.

" 'No more than that? Thank God! But what
are you going to do?'

" 'Nothing. And see that you say nothing about
it. It is hardly worth while making a fuss about it.
I will notify the police tomorrow.'

" 'You ought to do that tonight, after our guests have gone.'

" 'Well, I'll think it over.'

" 'Do you suspect any one?'

" 'No. But it is perfectly clear that the theft was committed by some person who has been in the house this evening. It is not a burglary in the usual sense of the word. I have taken a look at the extra men we hired. Whoever broke open the desk must have been a well-built, powerful fellow.'

" 'Do you know the extra help?'

" 'Yes, four of them,' answered the Captain. 'We have had them here before, but the fifth one, the fellow with the round, red face, is a new man. I don't like his eyes, and he has been peering around in an anxious kind of a way all evening long.'

"I was the man the Captain meant. The situation began to be uncomfortable. I had just about made up my mind to step up to husband and wife and let them know who I was, but that very moment they separated. And as the Captain left his wife, he whispered to her:

" 'Don't say a word about it!'

"I overheard the words distinctly."

"A few minutes passed, five in all, perhaps. People were deserting the little tables on the first floor where coffee had been served. From the second story sounded bursts of laughter, clapping of hands and loud applause. The comedian was giving his performance and all wanted to hear him.

"And then—in the midst of the little silence which followed one of these gusts of laughter, a heart-breaking cry suddenly rang out in the interior of the house.

"It seemed to come from the corner room in the southern wing of the building.

"It was succeeded by the loud report of a revolver.

"Following the shot the scream rang out again. A woman's voice cried:

" 'He is killing me!'

"For the space of a second not a sound was heard throughout the house, and then a terrible racket began.

"As I hurried in the direction of the screams I had heard, I looked at my watch. It was exactly eleven thirty-seven P. M.

"As you may imagine," Helgesen went on, "the shot and the cries caused a great commotion. The sound rang through the hall, with its great flight of steps, and penetrated into the second story. There Trybel was in the middle of one of his best humorous stories, and every one in the room rushed out to see what was the matter."

"I told you, I think, that I had been standing behind the great stair column in the hall, hidden by it.

I had heard plainly, beyond any chance of mistake, whence the shot and the cries had come—the corner room in the southern wing of the house. But Captain Karstens himself, at this mysterious moment, must have been somewhere nearby, for he ran through the rooms ahead of me.

"When we reached the corner room we at once smelled powder-smoke.

" 'Lock the door!' the Captain called out to me.

"I knew what was in his mind. He did not want the guests crowding into the room before he himself had found time to get an idea of what had happened.

"Against a chair lay a young girl in a faint, the lower part of her body stretched out along the floor.

"The Captain bent over her.

" 'It is Maja,' said he. His voice was grave, but he showed not a trace of nervousness. That Karstens is a mighty cold-blooded proposition.

"He listened to the girl's breathing and felt her pulse.

" 'Well, she has not been murdered,' he then remarked.

"Suddenly he drew himself up and rushed at me:

" 'Don't stand there like a dummy! Go fetch a doctor! Make yourself useful!'

" 'It would be better,' I said to him, 'to catch the criminal.'

"And with that I pointed to the floor, where a little Browning revolver lay gleaming in the light of the electric bulbs.

"In front of the locked door the astonished murmurs of the guests came to our ears.

"As you know, my dear Krag, I have fooled around a bit with medicine. It was easy for me to make sure that the young lady had only fainted, probably from fright, and that she was not even wounded, let alone murdered.

"I went out into the hall, fetched some cold water, and calmed the excited guests, telling them that the whole thing was merely a mysterious misunderstanding, and that nothing at all had happened."

"When the young lady regained her senses I found out that she was Mrs. Karstens' maid. Still quite confused, she opened her eyes, looked at the wall in a horrified manner, and made an attempt to flee. Captain Karstens had to hold her back by force. It was plain that she had lived through something which had terrified her in the highest degree.

" 'You must try and calm yourself,' the Captain told her. 'Tell us what happened to you. . . .' "

Here Helgesen stopped talking. He drew a little sketch on paper and passed it over to Krag.

"It is necessary for you to take a closer look at the house. I have drawn a cross to mark the position of the corner room. That is where the dramatic scene took place. The door to the left is the one against which the guests crowded in order to get in. The door to the right led into the bedroom, and was locked while the party was going on.

"It was to this bedroom door that Maja pointed, whispering timidly:

" 'That way, that way!'

"Then it seemed as though she were about to faint again, but Captain Karstens shook her, and kept her awake.

" 'He vanished that way,' she declared, trembling.

" 'Who?' asked the Captain.

" 'The man who fired the shot!'

"The Captain nodded to me.

" 'Take a look!' he said.

"I went to the door.

"It was locked. The key was in the key-hole, *on the inside!* So the door of the corner room had been locked from the inside and the key had been left in the lock.

" 'My dear Captain Karstens, look at this! The door is locked, and no one can walk through locked doors.'

" 'But I saw him disappear through that door,' the young girl insisted, stammering.

" 'Did you see him open the door?'

" 'No, but he disappeared. He glided *into* the door. And then I fainted.'

" 'What happened before that?' asked the Captain.

" 'I had come to the room to clear up and carry out the coffee-cups,' answered the girl. 'I thought there was not a soul in the room, when suddenly a figure rose up in front of me.'

" 'A man?'

" 'Yes, a tall, dark man wearing a hat and an overcoat.'

"She gave a closer description of the man she had seen.

"No, she never had seen him before, either at Karstens' or anywhere else. He had a dark, full beard, small eyes, wore gold-rimmed eye-glasses, and seemed to be about thirty-five years of age. He was well dressed.

"Suddenly, she told us, he threatened her with a revolver and said: 'If you make a move I'll shoot!'

"Then she had screamed for the first time. You know how poor, weak women act in such a case. They do not stop to think, they just scream.

"And then, the girl went on to tell, he shot at her and disappeared through the door. That was all she knew."

"Through the locked door?" asked Krag.

"That is what she says."

"But, my dear fellow, that's impossible. Were the windows locked?"

"Every last one of them," answered Helgesen, "locked from the inside."

"Then the man could only have left the room through the door which led to the drawing-rooms?"

"Yes."

"The same way both you and the Captain took when you came running up?"

"Yes."

"In other words, both of you must have seen the man who fired the shot!"

"Quite right."

"But since you did not see him, we find ourselves confronted by a very strange, one might almost say supernatural happening."

Krag smiled lightly. And Helgesen smiled as well.

"But the revolver?" Krag went on to ask. "The criminal was in such a hurry that he threw away his revolver?"

"Yes, we found it on the floor. It was a six-chambered model, and there still were five unused cartridges in it."

"And the bullet?"

"We could find no trace of it. I had the room searched very carefully, but there was not a sign of a bullet anywhere."

"That's strange."

"Very strange, and what became of the girl?"

"She was taken to her room, where she at once fell fast asleep. The whole thing must have been a great shock to her."

"And the guests? What did you tell the guests?"

"They were told that the girl had found a revolver and had accidentally fired the shot while handling it—nothing more."

"And how about yourself? You told me that Karstens suspected you of having had something to do with the theft of his two thousand crowns?"

Helgesen answered:

"While the young girl was still stammering out her broken explanations Karstens gave me a keen glance and then said: 'No paid servant acts as you do. He would not say, "My dear Captain."'

"'You are quite right,' I replied, 'I am not a servant.'

"I showed him my police shield, and in a few words explained the situation to him. He seemed very much taken back when he read the mysterious letter we had received at police headquarters."

"Yes, and now let us get back to the letter," said Krag. "If I understand you correctly, we are not yet through with the happenings at No. 54 Pine Street."

"No, for no sooner had the Captain succeeded in quieting his guests than he came to me in a great state of excitement and said: 'There has been a second robbery!'

" 'Here in the house?' I asked him.

" 'Yes, in my wife's boudoir.'

" 'What has been stolen?'

" 'Jewelry worth five thousand crowns!' "

Helgesen was about to go on when Krag interrupted him with a surprising remark:

"Aha, now I begin to see the connection!"

Helgesen rose, very much astonished.

"You really have a clue? That is more than I can say, after an investigation of several days."

"There is just one question I should like to ask you," Krag continued, quite unmoved. "Or, rather, there are a few facts I should like to have clearly established."

He gave another glance to the sketch Helgesen had drawn for him.

"The corner room in which the shot was fired lies in the southern wing of the house?"

"Just so."

"And Mrs. Karstens' room, from which the jewels were stolen, lies in the northern wing?"

"That is right. Did you guess it?"

"No, I say so because it should be according to a calculation of probabilities," Krag replied. "Have you arrested the girl?"

"Which girl?"

"The chamber-maid, of course. Maja was her name, was it not?"

"But why on earth should we arrest this poor, frightened young woman at whom some one had been shooting?"

"Tell the truth," said Krag, "did you never even suspect her the least little bit?"

"At first I suspected every one of the Captain's servants, male and female. You may rest assured that each and every one of them was given a thorough going-over. But we did not find the least cause for suspicion; all were able to give a valid alibi. And the best alibi of the lot was that of the chamber-maid Maja."

"How so?" Krag asked with seeming curiosity. Yet the knowing smile which played about his lips as he asked showed that he already had guessed what Helgesen was about to tell him.

"Mrs. Karstens," Helgesen replied in a decided tone of voice, "informed me that she was in her boudoir at the moment the shot was fired. At that time the theft had not taken place. She had just taken off some of the jewels she had worn around her neck at dinner when, frightened by the shot, she had hurried from the room. When she returned, half-an-hour later, the robbery had been committed. You must admit that under those circumstances it would be very hard indeed to cast suspicion on her young maid."

"All that you say agrees perfectly with my own

deductions," Krag replied. "Are you sure that Maja is still in Captain Karstens' service?"

"We can easily find out," said Helgesen, taking up the telephone. A moment later he had the information he wanted. Maja the chamber-maid had left the Karstens a few days before.

Helgesen was evidently at a loss. Where had she gone? To take a place in the home of General Consul Baldrigg, on Drammes Road.

Helgesen rang up the General Consul.

No, they had no girl by that name. In fact, they had not engaged a new servant for some months.

"You see," said Krag, "Maja has disappeared. If you can find her you will have one end of the knot to be unraveled in your hand."

As he spoke Krag moved closer to the table.

"Now I will show you how the whole thing happened.

"Maja was an accessory to the robbery. What she did made the robbery possible.

"The thief, with unparalleled impudence, undertook to work in a house swarming with guests. In order to carry out his robbery successfully all he needed was to be alone and unobserved for a moment.

"But he had to make sure that there would be no one in Mrs. Karstens' room.

"So he calculated that if by some trick he could

manage to send host, hostess and all their guests to the southern wing of the great house, he would be able to work for a few minutes in the northern wing without being disturbed.

"To do this he needed a helper.

"And if you will telephone once more and inquire, you will be told that innocent Maja had not been in Captain Karstens' service more than a month.

"It was Maja's business to fire off the revolver in the corner room and to scream.

"Oh, yes, you need not look surprised! It was Maja who fired the shot.

"There were six cartridges in the revolver; the first which she fired was a blank cartridge; the others, which were left, were all loaded.

"And, that explains why the revolver lay on the carpet. After firing the shot, the young woman threw it away.

"Her fantastic story about the strange man was all pure invention. In fact it was a stupid falsehood and one easily enough disproved.

"But the noise she made brought about the desired result: it called every one in the house to her.

"The thief took advantage of the favorable opportunity when one side of the house was empty for a few minutes.

"Mrs. Karstens rushed from her room. The

thief went in, put the jewels in his pocket, and then mingled with the other guests.

"I am sorry to have to tell you so, my good friend, but the answer to the riddle seems a very simple one."

Helgesen nodded. The chief of police smiled, pleasantly surprised.

"And yet your answer has one very weak point," said Helgesen.

"What is it?"

Helgesen handed Krag the list of Captain Karstens' guests.

It was headed by Bishop Moosgard, and ended with retired State Counsellor Knold. The names were all names of well-known and distinguished people.

"I have made certain," said Helgesen, "that the thief could not have been one of the servants. All of them have proved their innocence. I will admit that Maja the chamber-maid is revealed in rather a curious light, but would you honestly venture to say, after reading the list of distinguished men and women I have just given you, that one of them must be the thief?"

Krag answered evasively.

"Do you recall an old story," he asked, "about a robbery which was once committed at a society affair? Only the very highest social circles were represented, but the host was a foreigner, yet when he discovered that he had been robbed, he made no bones about it, and in spite of his guests' lively protests, he had them all searched."

"Yes, I remember the case."

"And the stolen articles were found on the person of a lady of the highest social standing. The scandal was hushed up, but some information regarding it leaked out. And now I really do not know with which name on your list I ought to begin. But I give you my word that if Captain Karstens had been less the gentleman and more the foreigner on the evening he was robbed, he would have recovered his gold and his jewels."

"That is a rather terrible suspicion you express, my dear Krag," interposed the Chief of Police. "Do you mean to carry on your hunt for the thief by following that trail?"

"That is what I expect to do."

"Then I hope that you will proceed only with the greatest caution, since otherwise we may easily be involved in a scandal. How are you going to begin?"

"The only thing to do," replied Krag, "is to investigate the guests in the order given. I shall commence with the bishop."

"And then take the general?"

"Exactly. And after him the old professor."

"It sounds like a fairy-tale," remarked the Chief dubiously.

"I think it is a fairy-tale," answered Krag. "And now I must be going. Do nothing more before six o'clock. I shall be back by then!"

At six 'clock Asbjörn Krag was back in the office of the criminal police division. He was in evening dress and slightly disguised, so slightly that, though his friends might recognize him, any chance acquaintance would consider him a perfect stranger.

"You have been busy for several hours," said the Chief of Police. "Have you discovered a clue?"

"Unfortunately, I had to break off a most interesting investigation," was Krag's reply.

"Why?"

"Because I have to go to a dinner party, as you may see."

"Ah, I suppose it is some important family council?"

"No, it is an ordinary, everyday dinner party at Consul Birger's house."

"I did not think you cared enough about dinner parties to let them interrupt an interesting investigation," said the Chief of Police, a little huffed.

"I do not," was Krag's answer, "but when I have a chance of meeting the man from No. 54 Pine Street, I am willing to run the risk of being bored at a dinner such as the one in question."

CHAPTER II

ASBJORN KRAG was one of the first among Concul Birger's guests to arrive. He was at once introduced to the famous specialist in sleeping sickness, Dr. Sydow, who had returned from the Congo only a short time before, as a friend of the Consul's, and the doctor immediately engaged Krag in a conversation about the Congo to which the detective could return only vague and unsatisfactory answers. He was glad when one by one other guests began to arrive. It was a men's party dinner.

Krag knew what these evenings at Consul Birger's were like. They began with an excellent dinner. The dinners served in the Birger home had a reputation among all lovers of good cheer in the city. Everything was done in first-class style. At dinner champagne was usually the only wine drunk, so that the guests soon were in the best of possible moods. Dinner usually ended toward eleven o'clock. Then coffee was served, and there was some general conversation until twelve, when liqueurs and whisky were passed.

This was the signal for the beginning of the party proper.

That is to say, it could hardly be called a "party."
The gentlemen sat down at small tables and cards
were produced. Consul Birger played only with
good card players.

He himself, though he could not be called wealthy,
had investments which gave him a large enough in-
come to allow him to indulge his passion for high
play. He was one of the best card-players in the
city, and enjoyed all games of chance, yet poker was
his favorite. His preference for poker he had
brought with him from America, where he had lived
for a time, and it was one he never had abandoned.
Perhaps he never had tried to do so. Poker was his
relaxation. The tension of the game refreshed him
when he was tired of business. For Consul Birger
did not gamble in order to win money: he played
only for the excitement of the game. Yet in order
to secure this element of suspense the stakes had to
amount to a sizeable amount. That their gains and
losses might amount to a few thousands one way or
another did not disturb any of these gentlemen who
played. Incidentally, the rules of the game were
very strictly observed. One fixed rule was that the
game—no matter how it stood—must end promptly
at three-thirty, and not a minute later.

Birger had his regular poker evening once a week,
usually on Saturdays. The same people did not always come, but certain ones, his most intimate

friends, were his main reliance. And it was these very men who were present this evening. Mrs. Birger, who at larger entertainments was an ideal hostess, did not appear on these poker evenings, but kept her room. The Consul had no children, and this may have been one of the reasons why he enjoyed a game of cards from time to time in his home. He never visited restaurants.

Little by little, the players gathered on this evening. The most distinguished among the guests was evidently young Professor Winger, a very famous philologist, specializing in ancient languages. He was a man who had travelled extensively, very amiable and animated, with the gift of talking with any one and every one in an interesting and agreeable fashion. Then there was the big real estate operator, Gressen, who was reputed to be a millionaire one day and as poor as a churchmouse the next. Besides there was Dr. Birkelund, son of old Professor Birkelund; Captain Stangenberg, a rich, easy-living cavalry officer; the composer, Binge, who once in the dim past had composed an opera and had since been living on the fortune he had inherited, and, finally, Asbjörn Krag and Consul Birger himself.

Before the dining-room door was opened Birger improved the opportunity of exchanging a few words with Krag in the hall, words which showed that they were old acquaintances.

"I hope I shall see you here oftener after this," said the Consul. "I had no idea that you would be interested in a little everyday evening of poker."

"Well, call it a new hobby of mine," answered Krag. 'After all, what is there for a man to do in this tiresome town? I must have a little change, a little excitement, or I will have to take to morphine."

"But why don't you want me to introduce you by your right name?"

"For the same old reasons I had in the past. I wish to remain unknown."

"Among these honest people?"

"Among these honest people most of all," replied Krag, while his eyes sparkled humorously. "What do you suppose they would say if they suddenly found out that you had introduced a private detective in your little poker club? At the very least they would think you had strange ideas."

"Not at all," said the Consul, eagerly, "they would be very much interested in making your acquaintance, especially if I told them of the brilliant stroke which made us acquainted with each other."

"Sh!" whispered Krag. "Here comes Dr. Sydow. He will begin to talk about the Congo again. What on earth can I tell him about the Congo that he does not already know? He thinks he has to be polite. If only he had chosen some other country. However . . ."

"Saved!" cried the Consul and clapped his hands. At his signal the door of the dining-room was opened, and the little company filed in, all talking animatedly as they went.

The champagne was served with the caviar, and the guests expanded visibly under its influence. Fortunately nothing more was said of the Congo. In some mysterious way the conversation had been turned on the social events of the season. Asbjörn Krag had only dropped a word here and there, and yet it was he who with masterly skill had turned the table-talk in the direction it had taken. He wanted to find out how much or how little was known by the guests about the robberies which already had taken place.

"There can be no doubt," said Dr. Birkelund, "that something has been hushed by which must have happened at Karstens' last evening affair."

"At any rate the story he gave out was rather hard to swallow," remarked Dr. Sydow. "He claimed the chamber-maid was handling a revolver. —Do you know what they say?"

His query was received with general silence. All those present seemed to know exactly what had been said.

"They say," the thick-skinned doctor continued, not at all put out, "that there was a burglar in the corner room."

"And that the chamber-maid shot at him?" added Dr. Birkelund, with a mysterious smile.

"At any rate," the real estate man threw in, "one thing is certain: a robbery took place that night at Captain Karstens. I got that much from the police themselves."

"A fine police force," said Doctor Sydow, "that never discovers anything!"

And turning to Asbjörn Krag he added:

"No doubt you are used to seeing the police act with greater firmness and rapidity, since you have travelled so much in the great countries of the world?"

Krag nodded.

Gressen, who was keen for a sensation, did not feel like letting the subject drop.

"I spoke to Karstens later," he said, "and the Captain was quite strange and secretive about it. He has changed. It looks as though he had received some sudden shock. And he denies positively that any robbery took place. His denials give the whole matter a very mysterious look. It is possible, even . . ."

"Sh, sh!" came from several sides at once, "let us talk about something else!"

"What I mean," Gressens went on, somewhat uncertainly, "is that it is quite possible Karstens discovered the thief, and that the discovery depressed him. He does not want a scandal. But who can the thief be? Yes, who, gentlemen? There were a large number of guests present that evening. I did not know half of them."

But now the talkative and inquisitive real estate man was told that he had said enough, and the host introduced another topic of conversation.

Toward eleven the gentlemen gathered in the smoking-room for coffee. Their host, Consul Birger, stood in one corner of the room, talking with Asbjörn Krag. He mentioned the real estate man's lack of tact. "He has too lively an imagination," he said, "but otherwise is a very intelligent man. The only thing to do is to interrupt him in good season, for otherwise he is apt to make all sorts of *faux pas."*

Asbjörn Krag answered only in words of one syllable, while his eyes strayed around the room.

Suddenly the Consul noticed his absent-mindedness.

He looked at him for a moment in silence.

"What is the matter?" he then asked.

"Nothing," was Krag's answer.

The Consul suddenly grew pale.

"My God," he cried, "I have a terrible suspicion!"

"Suspicion? How so?"

"You are not a card-player at all!"

"That happens to be the truth."

"You did not come here to play."

"Yes, I did. I came here to take part in a game which—for me at any rate—is more interesting than all the poker-parties in the world."

The Consul betrayed his surprise by a gesture.

"Be quiet," said Krag. "There is nothing to worry about."

"But what was your object in coming here?"

"To play—as I said."

"Do you really mean to play with us?"

"Of course."

"But we play a stiff game."

Krag smiled.

"Your game will not be stiff enough to make me lose my nerve."

Yet the Consul had grown uneasy. He cast sly glances at the company, chatting happily, made up entirely of his friends. Asbjörn Krag stood as he had been standing, watching them, weighing one man after another. Birger found it impossible to explain his interest, since nothing had happened to arouse it. How strange Krag's sudden appearance in this gathering was, in any case. The whole matter was very strange. At the moment Birger's greatest fear was that Krag would betray his identity, and that it would become known that he, the Consul, had smuggled in a detective at one of his card-parties. What a stir it would make in Christiania! What a morsel it would be for the scandal-mongers! Krag seemed to divine Berger's thoughts, for as he passed him he whispered in his host's ear:

"Do not worry! I shall see to it that nothing happens!"

But the detective's parting remark convinced the Consul of two things: first, that something was not in order; secondly, that Krag would do all he could to avoid a scandal and that he could depend on him in that connection.

Then he tried to think which one of his guests could have excited the detective's interest.

And mentally he passed his guests in review, one by one. As he did so a chill ran down his back. Why, the persons present were one and all well-known people, men of fortune and of reputation, men holding good positions, influential business men! If anything had happened it certainly could not be a question of money.

Perhaps Krag did not have the guests in mind at all, but only the servants.

Yet Krag seemed to pay no attention whatever to the servants. He was interested only in the guests.

Such were Consul Birger's thoughts as he stood waiting for the gentlemen to give the signal for the game to begin.

At that very moment the Consul's old valet was arranging the card-tables in the large salon. The company was to be divided into two separate groups of players.

Gradually the gentlemen present began to drift toward the tables.

Liqueurs were served, and every one grew more animated and began to look forward expectantly to the excitement in store for him.

None dreamed that their expectancy was to be gratified in a manner till then unknown in any poker club in Christiania.

The Consul's old valet was given the money for the chips in advance, and paid the gentlemen who won their winnings. He was the banker for the game.

He now posted himself beside the large box of colored chips and said:

"Gentlemen, the game is opened!"

The old valet had to repeat only two simple sentences on the evenings when cards were played. The one was his announcement that the game was opened. The other sentence was to the following effect: "Gentlemen, please cash in your chips!"

Gressens, the real estate operator, was one of the most enthusiastic players, hence he was the first one to seek out the chip-box.

Putting his hand in his coat-pocket for his bill-fold, he ordered—four one hundred crown chips, three fifty crown chips, and the remainder of his crowns in ten crown chips.

"What a nuisance," he mumbled, "I must . . .

Suddenly he grew quite excited and commenced to dig in all his pockets.

Then he looked very serious.

"What a nuisance," he mumbled, "I must have laid it down again by the mirror!"

He glanced at the guest standing beside him, Dr. Sydow.

"Have you forgotten your bill-fold, old man? In that case you must let me . . ."

"Thanks," answered Gressens. "I must have left my bill-fold on the table with the mirror. I hope I have not lost it. I have nearly five thousand crowns in it."

"Only absent-minded ladies ever lose their money," said Dr. Sydow, jokingly. "Let me supply you with chips. I want just what you asked for, so all that is necessary is for me to double your order. Let me have eight one hundred crown chips, Jean, six fifties and the rest in small chips!"

Jean began to count out the red, blue and yellow chips, and Dr. Sydow put his hand in his pocket.

But he kept it there, and then began to sniff the air as though he suddenly had made a most remarkable discovery.

When he took his hand from his pocket it was empty.

"Well, this is a caution!" he cried. "It is the strangest thing that has happened to me in the course of my whole life. I have forgotten my bill-fold, too!"

"Impossible!" said every one. "Look in your other pockets! It must be in one of them!"

Dr. Sydow went through all his other pockets, but without any result.

The situation began to grow amusing, and the other men commenced to smile.

Consul Birger came forward and said that of course he would be glad to accommodate both his guests with any amount they might wish to have.

"How much?" he asked with a smile, putting his hand in his pocket. "How much would you . . ."

But the remainder of the sentence stuck in his throat and he suddenly turned pale.

"Jean," he said to his valet, "go to my room and see whether I left my bill-fold lying on the table."

A chorus of laughter greeted his words. But the Consul wore a sickly expression.

"You are joking, Birger!" every one shouted. "You are piling on the agony! You have your bill-fold in your pocket this very minute!"

But the Consul only shook his head, and insisted that such was not the case. And the expression of

his face would have convinced the most unbelieving
Thomas that he was telling the truth.

Jean, the taciturn old valet, soon came back shak-
in his old grey head. He had found no bill-fold.

And now the situation grew tense, and all joking
came to an end.

Suddenly a voice called out:

"Gentlemen, let us all look in our pockets!"

It was the voice of Asbjörn Krag.

His suggestion was hardly necessary, for by this
time the hand of every man present was in his
pocket.

The moment after the whole company, which
had been so full of good spirits and jollity, presented a most peculiar spectacle of surprise and
puzzlement.

A few of the gentlemen stood hesitating, their
hands in their pockets.

Others dug in their clothes like mad.

And from every corner of the room sounded the
cry:

"I too! I too! Did anything like this ever happen before?"

Then, suddenly, another voice fell in, and said:
"But not I!"

It was Asbjörn Krag. He showed his bill-fold
whose contents he had examined. It had not been
touched.

Even Asbjörn Krag was surprised, very much surprised, and he could not conceal his astonishment.

His host looked timidly from one guest to the next, but it was at Asbjörn Krag that he looked longest.

The professor of philology now spoke:

"Gentlemen, we might as well admit the truth. We have been robbed!"

There were cries of astonishment.

"Robbed? But by whom? And where? When?"

The questions crossed in the air. Every one was talking at once.

Krag interposed.

"Since I am the only one among you who has not been robbed, I venture to suggest that we lock the doors!"

Yet at that very moment one of the younger servants appeared with a letter on a silver card-tray.

"It is a letter for Mr. Asbjörn Krag. He is supposed to be among the gentlemen here."

"Asbjörn Krag?" There were murmurs of astonishment. "The detective? But he cannot be in here!"

Yet the diguised detective at once took and opened the letter.

"I am Asbjörn Krag," he said.

The letter contained a bank-note for a hundred crowns, and a card.

The card read:

"In order that the gentlemen may not go short of change for their taxi-fares I enclose herewith one hundred crowns.

"Very respectfully,
"The Man of the Villa Rosenhain."

The last few minutes had been full of surprises. Now a silence fell, and the eyes of every guest were fixed on Asbjörn Krag, who stood quietly reading aloud the strange message he had received. He held the one hundred-crown note in his hand.

After Krag had studied the card carefully he turned to his host:

"Call the servant!"

Birger hesitated.

But now the other guests began to crowd forward.

"A detective in the house!" cried Dr. Sydow. 'Why, it's scandalous!"

The perspiration of terror broke out on Consul Birger's forehead. He was pale with excitement.

"I knew it," he murmured, "I knew it. Now a scandal is unavoidable."

"Call the servant," repeated Asbjörn Krag.

The Consul rang.

Then he turned to his guests and said: "Gentlemen, I trust we are the victims of some mystifica-
tion, some practical joke."

"Do you happen to have a parlor magician in
your house, too?" asked the real estate man with a
fixed stare.

"Not that I know of," answered Birger, "but I
will not guarantee it. It looks as though anything
might happen today."

The servant came in. He was a young fellow
who only had been in the Consul's service for a
few months. He did not look as though he were
very bright.

"Who brought this letter?" Krag asked.

"A young lady," answered the servant.

"Did she speak Norwegian?"

"Yes, sir."

"What did she say?"

"She said I was to deliver the letter to the person to whom it was addressed. I told her that no
one by that name lived here. Then she said: 'Oh,
yes, just take it in to the company. The gentleman
is in the house.' And then she went off."

Krag looked at the fellow.

Then he asked: "Was she pretty?"

"She was young and very pretty, sir."

"Very well. You can go," said Krag. The
servant left.

When he had gone, Asbjörn Krag turned to the company: "I owe you gentlemen an apology," he said.

"You surely do! Quite right! And without delay!" were the exclamations that arose around him. It was clear that now Birger's guests were not thinking so much of the money they had lost, as of the circumstance that the Consul had admitted a professional detective into their company in disguise.

"It is not alone true that I am a detective," said Krag, "but also that you gentlemen have been robbed by the cleverest thief who ever operated in Christiania. The affair is all the more interesting since it may turn out that this uncommonly clever thief is a very pretty, young girl. At any rate, in some mysterious way the thief managed to find out that I was among you. And he spared me. He showed me a consideration I do not deserve, for I have let him get the better of me in the most shameful manner. I take the liberty of calling your attention to the fact that I sought out this company in order to catch the thief."

"Which thief?" every one cried with astonishment. "Who is the thief of whom you are talking?"

"I am talking of the thief," Krag answered, "who has been operating in Christiania for the past few months, of the thief whom you gentlemen were discussing at dinner. I am talking of the thief who stole Captain Karsten's jewels."

"And you expected to find him here?" asked the profess of Egyptology.

"Yes," Krag replied, "but that is not the worst."

"Then what is the worst?"

"The worst is that I have met him here."

"You mean that he has been here?"

"I am convinced of it."

"Here in my home?" the Consul burst out.

"If you gentlemen will give the matter a moment's thought," Krag answered, "you will see that I am right. You all have been robbed. Where are your bill-folds, gentlemen?"

"Yes, our bill-folds!" said the guests as their hands mechanically slid into their pockets. "They are gone!"

"Just so. Hence there are only two possibilities. Either you gentlemen were robbed on your way here, or else you were robbed in the house. In the first event it would be useless to hunt for the thief. In the second case it is not impossible that he still may be in the house. I hope my order to have doors locked has been obeyed!"

"The doors are locked," the Consul declared.

"In that case, gentlemen, I shall be obliged to question you, one at a time. So far as you are concerned, Captain, you probably came in your own auto?"

"Yes," replied the cavalry officer.

"And you, Dr. Sydow?"

"I came in a taxi."

"Did you pay at the door?"

"Yes."

"Are you sure that you still had your bill-fold at the time?"

"Yes. I paid the chauffeur with a five-crown note. My money was in my bill-fold. And now change and bill-fold both are gone. I have been robbed of two thousand crowns, more than I can afford to lose.

"What you tell me is of the greatest importance," remarked Krag. "You confirm what I already had taken for granted, that the theft must have been committed here in this house."

"Yet that is impossible!" cried the guests.

"Nothing is impossible," replied the detective solemnly. "I can assure you, gentlemen, that we have to deal with an exceptionally daring and cunning criminal. And this criminal has a sense of humor, as is proved by the letter I received."

Krag once more read the letter, and the wonder of the listeners grew.

"It was written several hours ago," said he. "I can see that quite clearly by the ink. Hence the criminal had planned everything in advance. The letter was ready to hand to me. After he had made his haul, he had it delivered."

"Suppose we assume," Krag continued without interruption, "that the robbery was carried out here in the building. Since no stranger was present, the crime must have been committed by one of the Consul's servants. . . ."

"I will answer for my servants," interrupted Consul Birger.

"Very well," answered Krag. "In that case it must have been one of *us!*"

There was laughter. There was loud laughter. Some of the guests quite evidently still thought that the whole thing was a hoax of some sort.

One of them cried:

"If one of us is the thief, then you must be the one, for you are the only person who has not been robbed!"

Krag heard the accusation with the greatest calmness.

"For a moment I wondered myself whether I were the thief or not."

"He must be crazy!" everybody said.

Asbjörn Krag was well aware of the fact that the company was growing more and more angry. The men were not only enraged to think that they had been victimized by so daring a robbery, but they were still more indignant at the scandal which threatened them. And this accounted for the painful silence which suddenly fell. The whole thing seemed so fantastic that they did not know whether to think they were the victims of a practical joke, or whether they really had been robbed. And Krag, aware of this uncertainty, and himself bewildered, was only trying to gain time. A few minutes, half an hour, would give him a chance to pick up a clue. That was why he tried to keep the party occupied with conversation. But he now saw that this would not do, and that he would have to declare himself.

He began:

"Gentlemen, during the past few months we have been victimized by a very bold and cunning criminal. I must admit, gentlemen, that I suspected this criminal might be found among the very persons who met here this evening as they have been in the habit of doing for some time."

A murmur of annoyance replied to Krag's remark.

"Do not misunderstand me," Krag hastened to say, "a detective cannot make distinctions. When his suspicions are aroused, when anything puzzles him, it is his duty to suspect one and all. I admit that none of you here present could have committed the robbery. (Noise and murmurs of indignation.) This letter which I just received has convinced me that the thief already has left the house. Eight of us came here, and eight of us still are present. We have been in each other's company the whole time ever since we arrived, and no one has left the house. If it turns out that none of us has the stolen money about him, then it is clear that the criminal must be looked for elsewhere, either among the servants, or—or——"

Here Krag hesitated.

"Or?" repeated the Consul.

"Or the robber is a man who is able to make himself invisible—and gentlemen, we might as well agree, once and for all, that the impossible is something which cannot happen."

Now the murmurs of indignation turned into an outburst of rage.

"My overcoat!" cried one. "My hat!" another. "Call my car!" said a third. On every side men exclaimed: "What impudence! He wants to search us! He must have lost his senses!"

Then the Consul intervened. He was pale and determined.

"I cannot allow a search," he said, "it would be an insult to my guests!"

Krag calmly seated himself in the nearest arm-chair.

"I regret," said he, "that I have often found myself obliged to permit myself insults of this kind."

And turning his head toward his friend the Consul he asked:

"Are the doors all locked?"

"Yes."

"Very well. Then there is nothing to prevent my having my way about this. I can assure you, gentlemen, that I know absolutely nothing at this moment. But I insist on obtaining information, and I shall not be satisfied until my wish has been granted."

The Consul stepped up to him.

"How about your promise? Have you forgotten what you promised me? You said that there should be no scandal!"

"I promised that I, for my part, would cause no scandal," answered Krag. "You must admit, however, that chance has willed otherwise. And I have made up my mind not to yield unless something unforeseen happens to make it needless for me to search these gentlemen."

"And you really believe," queried the Consul, his face red with rage, "you really believe that one of *my* guests is in possession of the stolen money. It is an outrage!"

"I believe nothing, either one way or the other," replied Krag.

"But it is an insult!"

"Be that as it may. I must be certain. And in order to make things easier I shall begin with your servants. I noticed that you have two servants, a young man and an old one. Call them in. I will question the old man first. Were I any of you gentlemen, I would be glad to witness the scene, for it is full of exciting possibilities."

Two or three of the gentlemen sat down. There was laughter.

The Consul turned questioningly to his guests:

"Let him have his way about it," said the Professor of Egyptology. "The fellow is quite right. A search will be quite as interesting as a stiff game of poker."

With some reluctance the Consul pressed an electric button. He knew Krag, and knew that when Krag had made up his mind there was nothing to do but yield. Krag preferred the most terrible scandal and the most violent enmity to giving away a single inch.

The younger servant entered.

"Call Jean!" his master ordered. The Consul was a bit of a snob. He called his old valet Jean, though his real name was Lars Petersen. When the young man left the room, the gentlemen waited in silence.

Five minutes later the young servant returned, his face the picture of astonishment.

"I can't find Jean anywhere," said he. "I cannot understand it. I have searched the whole house, but he has gone; he must have run away."

The Consul started.

"Jean, old Jean, who has been my personal attendant for the last twenty years? . . . Impossible! Besides, it is *his* place to come when I ring twice!"

And the Consul jabbed the button like a man gone mad. The gentlemen whispered to each other: "Disappeared . . . Then he must be the one . . ."

"Impossible," insisted the Consul, and rang and rang again.

Suddenly a loud noise was heard outside. And before any one could make a move, the door was torn violently open, and a strange looking figure tottered into the room.

It was old Jean.

He seemed to have been in a fight. His clothes hung on him in disorder. His collar had been half torn from his neck. His white fair, usually so neat and smooth, stood up in tangled clumps on his head. His eyes stared wildly from beneath his bushy, overhanging brows.

"I heard . . . I heard you ring, sir," he stammered to the Consul, "just as I was coming in through the door. Why are the doors locked?"

He was almost ready to sink to the floor, and the Consul shoved him into an arm-chair.

There he sat for a time, hiding his face in his hands. It was clear that he was terribly excited, and that he must have experienced a great shock of some kind.

While cold water was being brought, Asbjörn Krag said to him:

"The doors? But you locked the doors yourself. Don't you remember our asking you to do so?"

The old servant looked up.

"You asked me to lock the doors, sir? When?"

"A few minutes ago. Or, to be exact, a quarter of an hour ago."

The old man shook his white head uncomprehendingly.

"A quarter of an hour ago," said he, "I was far away from here at that time."

Those present gathered around him. When they saw how terrified and confused he was, they completely forgot the insult offered them.

"Come, pull yourself together!" they said to Jean. "You are all upset. Do you mean to say you don't remember being here a quarter of an hour ago? Why, you waited on us all evening!"

After the old man had swallowed a glass of water he asked:

"Did I get here too late?"

"Too late for what?" asked his master.

"Too late for the party?"

The gentlemen looked at one another. It was plain that the old man did not know what he was saying. The Consul shook him. "You were here up to a minute ago," he said.

Evidently at a loss, and not grasping his meaning, the old man stared at the ground.

Now Krag once more intervened in the conversation.

"When did you leave the house?" he asked.

"When I received his letter," replied the old man, nodding in the Consul's direction.

"My letter?" said the latter. "I don't know what you are talking about!"

But Asbjörn Krag went on, quietly:

"When was that?"

"At five o'clock," was the old servant's answer. "And since that time I have not been here."

At that moment all could hear the telephone ringing in an adjacent room.

In a moment word came: "Telephone call for Mr. Asbjörn Krag!"

Krag went to the door, murmuring:

"That must be he—or she."

When Krag had left the room a general silence fell on the company. The tension among the guests had reached its highest point. All realized that chance had allowed them to share in a most unusual adventure.

Since Krag had not closed the door all could hear what was said at the 'phone. First Krag answered: "Yes," and then "Yes, it is I."

Krag did not know the voice at the other end

of the 'phone. It was a man's voice, low and rough. The person to whom it belonged was asking whether he had the honor of talking to the detective, Mr. Asbjörn Krag.

"Who are you?" Krag asked.

"The thief," answered the voice.

"The thief?"

The voice laughed. "The thief," it repeated. "I rang to call your attention to the fact that the box of poker-chips is behind the fire-screen."

"Which box of poker-chips?"

"The box of chips for the night's game. And now I regret that I can give you no further information. I am very sorry I was obliged to break up an interesting evening of poker, but I had no choice. You see, I needed the money!"

Asbjörn Krag could not help but laugh himself.

"Who are you?" he inquired.

"The thief," the voice replied once more, very seriously.

"But have you no other name?"

"Yes, I have as many names as there are days in the week, a new one for each day."

"What are you calling yourself today?"

"Today? Today my name is *Jean!*"

Asbjörn Krag started. He was about to say something when the other person rang off, and he could hear no more.

At once Krag called up Central, gave the signal call that put him in touch with police headquarters, and asked to be connected with the number he had been talking to that moment.

It was the 'phone exchange in the City Passage Building. The switch-girl answered him.

In reply to Krag's question she said that a gentleman had telephoned a moment ago, and then had left.

Could she describe him?

She could, exactly. He was an undersized man of middle age, with a grayish beard, and well dressed. She had heard him say quite plainly that he was the "thief," but he had laughed when he said "I" and she thought, of course, that he was joking.

Krag left the 'phone and returned to the smoking-room, where the gentlemen looked at him with curiosity. Old Jean had pulled himself together, and was standing.

"You look surprised," said the Consul. "Did you receive any important message by 'phone?"

"I must admit that I am surprised," Krag answered, "for I have been talking to the thief."

"With the lady who stole our money?" the cry went up. "What did she say? What did she want?"

"It was no lady," Krag replied, "it was a man. Our thief belongs to the male sex, but he had sev-

eral assistants, among them the pretty strawberry
blonde who brought the letter.   Yes, this infernal
robber had the unique impertinence to call me up on
the 'phone and pass the time of day."

"What did he want?"

"He only wanted to let me know where the poker
chips were," said Krag, pulling out the box from
behind the fire-screen." He is a polite rascal. I
look forward to meeting him and having an interesting chat with him."

Not one of Consul Birger's guests now thought
of leaving. They were all too much taken up with
these puzzling events which had succeeded each
other at such short notice.

But they were more at sea than ever as to how
the robbery had happened.

Krag, on the other hand, already had guessed.
He went up to old Jean, patted him on the shoul-
der in a comforting way and said:

"Well, old man, you must have had a good fright
after you had been called away."

"It was at five o'clock, just as I said," repeated
the valet.

"That may well be," answered Krag, "and later
you were not here?"

"No, I'm sorry to say," replied the old man,
"but I could not control my movements."

"I can understand that. Well, gentlemen, this

evening we all have had the honor of making the acquaintance of a very daring robber."

"But who was he?" was the question every one asked.

"He took Jean's place. And I can pay him the compliment of saying that he played his part well. On that head, our good, conscientious Jean need not worry a bit."

"But Jean was here!" cried the Consul.

"No," said Krag, "the man who waited on us was not Jean, but the thief himself. He was busy here masquerading as Jean, and very successfully took advantage of the fact that Jean is as silent as the grave when on duty. I can assure you gentlemen, that he must be a wonderful pickpocket. And I must admit I feel flattered to think he did not rob me. It proves that he is also a very careful person. Yes, I am afraid that all we can do is to resign ourselves to the facts. I will ask you to let me put a few questions to Jean in order to find out just what happened."

And Krag retired to the next room with the old servant, while the gentlemen remained seated in order to talk over the strange events of the evening. One consolation remained: they had not lost more money than they could afford to lose. They compared notes, and finally came to the conclusion that the daring sneak-thief had cleared between ten and eleven thousand crowns. It was a good bit of money.

Half an hour later Asbjörn Krag returned to the smoking-room in his overcoat.

All the others surrounded him in order to hear whatever news he might have gleaned.

He pulled out his watch. It was already eleven-thirty.

"I can spare just three minutes," he said, "in order to let you know what I have discovered.

"The thief, to judge by all the evidence, is a man at home in good society. Therefore I have every reason to believe that he has often been a guest of our friend the Consul at his poker evenings. Owing to the fact that he is an active member of good society he has gathered much information regarding people and conditions, which he is now using to advantage.

"He must be a well-bred, educated man, and he is a Norwegian.

"Probably he is not a professional criminal, but a man who, for some unknown reason, has been forced into a career of crime.

"From previous visits he knew that there would be a poker at Consul Birger's tonight. And he also knew that on such an occasion those present would be well provided with cash funds, and hence would offer a fine field for a venturesome pickpocket.

"At five o'clock, while the Consul was still in his office, the unknown robber sent a messenger to Jean. The messenger told the old servant that the Consul wanted to see him about some of the evening's details. Jean was called for in an auto, carried to a house near the Parkway, shut up in a room there, and guarded.

"Of course, the criminal had only hired this room —it was in a lodging-house—for a couple of days. It would be useless to look for a trace of him there.

"In the room of the Parkway house the servant was held by two of the thief's assistants, while he disguised himself, and appeared among the company as Jean. It was this false Jean who was ordered to lock the doors, and it goes without saying that he did so, but he also took good care to secure his booty and his own safety first."   -

"Then, only half an hour ago, the real Jean was set free.

"The rest you already know, gentlemen. It is very disagreeable to find that I have allowed myself to be fooled in such a way. Yet I am grateful for two things: First, that I have had the comparatively rare opportunity of measuring myself with a really bold, cunning thief, who has a sense of humor. And, secondly, that this case has given me a few clues which, sooner or later, may lead to some result."

Krag was on the point of going when he was again called to the 'phone:

"Telephone for Mr. Krag! From police headquarters!"

When Krag returned after a lapse of a few minutes he said with a smile:

"Gentlemen, I believe our mysterious friend has made up his mind to rob the whole town of Christiania. Now he has even robbed the Chief of Police!"

Silence, and then an outburst of laughter greeted the detective's words. And the tension of the exciting evening suddenly broke in a great gust of hilarity. The Chief of Police himself robbed! In the name of all that was holy, could a thief do more? And they laughed and laughed, but when some panted out a request for more details, Krag waived a goodbye and disappeared.

CHAPTER III

A T the next street corner he requisitioned a taxi and, breaking all speed laws, dashed to police headquarters.

He had expected to find the whole force in motion, because of the unusual theft, but all was quiet. He asked whether the Chief of Police was there, but no one could tell him definitely. However, he was taken to his office, and there sat the Chief at his big desk.

He was telephoning when Krag entered, and pointed to a chair. Krag seated himself.

And so he happened to hear the last words of the telephone conversation.

"Everything," said the Chief of Police, "every single, blessed thing, but do not mention it! If it is a joke we probably will get it back again, and if it is a real robbery we'll get it again, too!"

He hung up and stepped rapidly over to Asbjörn Krag.

"It is well you got here so quickly. Nothing like it ever has happened to me before. Can you imagine it? I have been robbed of about all I own in the world!"

The detective looked up at him in surprise.

"I will explain how the whole thing happened," said the Chief of Police. "I have just telephoned my wife, and she is quite out of her mind with astonishment. I have begged her to keep her mouth shut, for that is important. For the moment, you and I are the only ones on the force who know anything about it. It would make a fine story if the news spread that the Chief of Police himself had been robbed while he was looking for the mysterious robber!"

"Do you really believe it was the same man?"

"Yes."

"Have you anything to prove it?"

"Yes, a proof that cannot be questioned. I have his own testimony."

"Well, that promises to attract some attention," murmured Krag, as he began to take off his overcoat.

But the Chief stopped him.

"We'll only be here a moment," he said. "I just have a few orders to give. Did you come in an auto?"

"Yes, it is waiting."

"Good, then I can tell you everything while we are under way."

The Chief of Police gave a few orders to various subordinates, said that he would return in an hour, and then left the police building with Asbjörn Krag.

To the chauffeur he said:

"Bygdö Alley, No. 44!"

Asbjörn Krag seemed surprised. "We are bound for your home?" he said as they got in.

"My former home," the Chief of Police corrected him.

"I do not understand you. Have you moved?" Krag answered.

"No, but my *home* has been stolen."

The Chief of Police said this quite seriously, without changing countenance, and Asbjörn Krag's astonishment grew.

"A stolen home," remarked the detective. "That sounds odd, like a novel!"

"It really is a most romantic story, and probably the first and only instance in this country of a home having been stolen. It actually happened once in Moscow . . . Well, that is another story!"

Krag shook his head reflectively: "A whole house and lot?"

"No," said the Chief, "of course I mean only the furniture!" He looked at his watch. "We shall be there in five minutes, so I will use them to tell you what happened to me this evening at half after ten, that is to say, about two hours ago. As you may know, this summer, as in past years, I have been living out at Snarr Island. I move over there in the beginning of spring, and late in the fall I come back to town again. I motor out nearly every evening in my motor-boat, and since everyone is out on the island at this time, I usually go to a hotel instead of sleeping in my own house, when I am compelled to stay in town over night, for one or another reason. Naturally, from time to time, there is something to attend to at the house, and I can safely say that I go there about twice a week. I had planned to return to the city with my family in a few days, since it is beginning to grow cold. So this evening I thought I'd take advantage of an idle hour, go to the house, and see that everything was in order."

Asbjörn Krag, who now began to see where this was leading, asked:

"When were you there last?"

"Four days ago. Then I went there to look up some letters in my private desk."

"And everything was in order?"

"Not a thing had been disturbed. Well, at about ten-thirty I reached my house. As you know, I live on the ground floor. There was nothing to be noticed outside. The shades were down."

"Then you looked up at the windows?"

"Certainly, I looked up. You know at times one has some curious presentiments which one cannot explain. Everything was very quiet. It is a very quiet house. I unlocked the outside door, put the key into the lock of the hall door and stepped into the hall."

Krag interrupted him: "Had the lock been tampered with?"

"It was in perfect order. In the hallway I turned on the electric light. And there I had my first surprise. The hall was empty, and I recall saying to myself: Hello, some one has broken in! When I was there last, umbrella-stands and hatrack were there, now there was nothing to be seen. Only the lonely telephone stood on its stand. I felt a chill, but went on into the next room. And there I stopped short on the threshold, dumbfounded!"

"Was there nothing in the room?" asked Krag.

"No, and since I could not get a good idea in the dark, I turned on the light at once, and saw that the room had been stripped bare. I give you my word, there was not a bit of furniture, not a rug on the floor, not a picture on the wall. Do you know what my first thought was?"

"That you were dreaming."

"No, I thought I must have entered the wrong house. I must have gone up into the second story instead of stopping at the first, I thought. So I ran back quickly. But no, I really was on the ground floor; and there, beside the hall door, was my name on the door-plate.   Once more I rushed into the house."

"I went through all the rooms, and turned on the light everywhere.   Every room was empty, all the furniture wase gone.   Even the curtains had been taken down.   And things quite without value in themselves, like coal-scuttles and ash-trays, had disappeared."

"And the kitchen?"

"Well, at last I reached the kitchen.   And the kitchen was empty, too.   The only thing that had been left was a large pepper-box.   It stood in solitary majesty plumb in the middle of the kitchen table."

"It sounds like some well-planned practical joke."

"I'll not deny the fact.   I knew it was an intentional impertinence.   But the sight of that pepper-box at once removed all doubt as to whether I were in my own home or not.   For I do not believe there is a second pepper-box like it in town.   You are laughing?"

"I can't help it," said Krag, "the whole thing is too funny."

"I agree with you.   And when I stood in front of the pepper-box I had to laugh myself.   I think I laughed so loud that the people in the floor above could hear me.   Then I ran out and called the janitor."

"Was he surprised?"

"Not in the least. He merely asked whether I had forgotten something. 'Forgotten?' I said to him. 'Just step into my apartment with me, will you?' '*Your* apartment?' he queried in surprise, but came along. And as we stood in the middle of the empty apartment I asked him: 'Tell me, my dear fellow, am I living here or am I not living here?' "

" 'You?' he replied. 'No, you are not living here, for you moved out yesterday.' "

At that moment the taxi stopped in front of the house.

"Here we are," said the Chief of Police. "Come on into the house and I'll tell you the rest of this strange story."

"What interests me most," observed Krag, "is to discover how the thief made himself known to you."

"By letter," replied the Chief of Police. "By means of a typewritten letter, very neatly and politely expressed."

As both of them stood in the dark hallway, the Chief went on: "Wait a moment till I call the janitor. We must have him with us!"

Krag, who stood outside, waiting, heard his companion knock at one of the windows opening on the court, and a rude voice murmuring some indistinct reply.

"The janitor already has gone to bed," whispered

the Chief, as he returned, "but he will be here in
a minute. Have you a light, Krag?"

"Always!"

Krag pulled out his electric search-light, and
the Chief pointed to the walls of the hall. "Do you
see? The movers did not handle the things very
carefully. It is quite clear that they were in a
hurry. I wonder what my furniture looks like."

They both examined the dented plaster.

"I hope you will soon be able to form an idea
of the damage done to it," murmured Krag.

"I hope so, too," answered the Chief of Police,
laughing.

Now the janitor came up with a big lamp, and
Asbjörn Krag turned off his search-light. First the
Chief of Police showed him the hall door, which
Krag examined carefully without being able to find
the slightest trace of violence.

"It is an ordinary lock," he said, "and can be
opened without the least trouble."

Then they entered the long, inner hall.

"You must admit that my surprise was natural
enough," said the Chief of Police, "when I saw
my hall bare."

"Yes, I can understand it."

"And look at this!" The Chief opened the door
leading to the next room and they went right on.
Every room was empty, and only in the kitchen sat

the pepper-box, throned in lonely glory. Both men
could not help laughing once more.

Then the Chief of Police opened one of the
kitchen closet doors. "Here is my message," he
said and pointed to the inside of the closet. Krag
leaned forward and saw that a sheet of paper had
been pinned carefully to the wall. It bore the thief's
message.

"Have you touched the paper?" the detective
asked him.

"No, I merely read it."

But now the janitor bustled up. "Wait a minute, I'll get you the paper!" But Krag grabbed
his great, heavy fist. "Easy there!" Wait a minute, man, do you want to ruin the whole thing?"

Krag always carried a small case with him, no
larger than an ordinary bill-fold, in which he kept
a number of things of use to him in his investigations, among them a thin, colorless liquid which,
smeared on smooth surfaces, would hold and re-
tain finger-prints. The paper had been stuck up on
the wall with four thumb-tacks. Krag smeared the
liquid on the tacks, waited a few moments until it
had hardened, and then took the tacks from the
wall.

"If the criminal's fingers were only the least bit
sweaty," said he, "I ought to have a first-class means
of identifying him in about five or ten minutes."

Then he read the message on the paper. It was typewritten and said:
"Dear Sir:
Since you and your men have been unable as yet to discover the thief who is haunting the West End of town, you must not complain if his continued operations make you their victim. On the other hand, it is not the thief's intention to injure you beyond repair. He is willing to return to you certain articles which you may value highly. He is even prepared, under certain conditions, to return all you have lost. Should you desire an interview in this connection, the thief may be interviewed at the Continental Hotel, Room 14, on Friday the 29th, at three o'clock in the afternoon. I might call your attention to the fact that any display of force would interfere. Should any one else, beside yourself and one friend turn up at the conference, the thief will not put in an appearance.
                    Very respectfully yours,
            The Man of the Villa Rosenhain."
After Asbjörn Krag had carefully read this curious document, he took out the note he had received at Consul Birger's. Comparing both, he soon arrived at the conclusion that they had been written on the same paper, on the same machine, and with the same ribbon. There was no doubt about it. The thief who had sent Krag his note was the same

person who had tacked the impertinent letter on the kitchen closet wall.

"And now let us hear how the robbery occurred," said Krag, turning to the janitor, who had been watching his manoeuvres with the greatest surprise. "When were the things taken away?"

"Yesterday."

"How many loads were there?"

"Three. The first drove off at seven o'clock in the morning, and the last left at one-thirty in the afternoon. But it was one and the same van."

"Did it belong to some trucking firm?"

"No, there was no firm name on it. It must have been a private truck of some kind."

The Chief of Police nodded.

"I already have inquired among the trucking firms," he said, "and not one of them knows anything about a truck having been sent here."

"Did you never even suspect that there might be something out of order?"

"No, not at all. It often happens that the real estate people who have a house in charge do not notify me when some one is moving out. Besides, they brought a policeman along with them."

"A policeman?" said Krag, surprised. The Chief smiled. He already knew what had happened and the detective's atonishment amused him.

"Yes," said the porter. "A policeman in uniform

came with the movers, to see that everything was done according to law. It was patrolman No. 44. I often have had a chat with him. He told me that the Chief of Police had sent him, because he himself could not spare the time to come."

"And did he say why I had no time?"

"Certainly, he mentioned it accidentally. He said the Chief of Police was very busy laying his hands on a couple of impudent thieves who had made up their minds to plunder the whole city. That was why he had no time to give to his own business— so the Chief of Police said. And I must say that it all sounded like the Gospel truth."

"No doubt it did. How many furniture movers were there?"

"There were four, besides the patrolman. Big, strong fellows, between twenty and thirty. I never have seen men who went about their work in a livelier way. They just took the furniture—and off they were!"

"Well, well," said the Chief of Police.

"Yes, they tipped the grand piano over on edge, and shoved it through the door in a minute. All that broke off was a little bit of one leg, but that easily can be glued on again, so what difference does it make?"

The Chief of Police grew uneasy.

"Was the case damaged?" he asked.

"Of course," cried the janitor. "They just shoved the piano out, I tell you. But it does not seem to me that any real harm was done, just a few tones, perhaps, though it seemed to groan when they threw it into the truck."

"But what did the patrolman say when they abused the furniture in such a way?"

"Oh, he just looked on with a serious face, and said nothing at all. He made no objection. He did say, though, that when it come to moving, people had to take things as they found them. But, believe me, it all went off without much trouble. Excepting the big mirror."

"What happened to that?" the Chief of Police asked, nervously.

"Well, it was broken, so to say."

"The Chief of Police wiped the perspiration from his forehead. "Was anything else injured?" he asked.

"Not that I know of, but I can't say what happened to the hanging lamps and the big candelabra. For I was not around when they took them."

"Well, your news is not very reassuring to hear."

For the last few minutes Asbjörn Krag had been carefully looking at the thumb-tacks. Now he began to knock and blow off the brittle coat which covered them. Then he nodded, well pleased. On the first thumb-tack the impress of a thumb-print was plainly visible. Krag made a cornucopia out of a page of his note-book, carefully laid the thumb-prints into it, and put it into his pocket, together with the two letters.

Then he asked for a description of the four furniture movers, and the janitor, who seemed to have a pretty good memory, gave him the necessary information.

"And what shall we do now?" asked the Chief of Police.

"Accept the invitation," answered Krag.

"What do you mean? Do you really think we will find the thief at the Continental Hotel?"

"Yes, under certain conditions."

"What are they."

"I can tell you exactly under which conditions we will *not* catch sight of him," was Krag's answer.

"You mean to say . . . ? Suppose we went there in force, and posted police in all the passages and in the street? They could be disguised."

"You under-estimate the mysterious gentlemen with whom we have to deal. He will see through it at once, and will simply not be there."

"So you think we two ought to go alone?"

"Yes."

"Supposing it is a trap?"

"I wish it were," answered Krag.

At that moment he looked at the kitchen window,

and gave a start. He had seen something outside in the dark, and stood there with a surprised expression, pointing to the window. Its four panes were filled with the dark blackness of night, but in the left lower pane showed a pale human face, which suddenly disappeared.

"Into the hall!" cried the Chief of Police.

But Krag already was in the corridor. Yet as he opened the hall-door he heard rapid footsteps on the wooden floor of the outer hall entrance, and realized that he had come too late. The curious owner of the face already had gone his way. Krag stepped out into the street.

Bygdö Alley lay silent and deserted. On the far side of the street a few cabs and taxis were moving by, and in one of the side streets a boy was whistling a popular tune. Otherwise all was wrapped in the darkness and quiet of night. The detective saw that for the moment any attempt at pursuit would be useless. There was absolutely no clue as to which direction the stranger had taken. Besides, it was not even certain that the owner of the face was the mysterious thief. He might have been an accidental sneak-thief of some sort.

Before Krag re-entered the empty apartment, he stood for a moment lost in thought. Then he locked the house-door when he stepped inside. If there were any more mysterious beings on the ground floor, they now were safely locked in.

In the hall he found the Chief of Police and the janitor. The latter was very much excited.

"That was one of them," said he. "I could never forget those black eyes!"

Krag understood what he meant. But, nevertheless, he asked:

"One of them? What do you mean by one of them?"

"One of the furniture movers, of course," the janitor went on. "The fellow who flung the piano into the truck."

The Chief of Police shook his fist.

"I wish I had him here," he muttered. "I'd show him something about flinging. Did he get away, Krag?"

"Without leaving a sign," the latter answered, as he returned to the kitchen.

There he stood for a moment and looked disguestedly at the black window. "It is quite evident," he said, indistinctly, "that we have made a mistake there."

The Chief of Police looked a question and Krag pointed to the window.

"We forgot to cover it, or put a man on guard outside—to take any precaution. We have been spied upon. These people can see us quite plainly."

"Nonsense! We have done nothing which could

possibly interfere with the success of our investigations. Besides, we now have a reliable identifica-
tion. You got a good look at the fellow?"

"Yes, I noticed how he was disguised.

"Disguised?"

"Yes, for I do not believe that his gray hair and
beard, and his young, fiery eyes were mates."

"In other words," said the Chief of Police, with
a sarcastic smile, "everything that happens only
serves to show how greatly they are ahead of us."

"Beyond question," said Krag with emphasis.
"But come, let us go! We can do nothing further
by artificial light. Tomorrow you must send a man
here. It may be possible for him to secure a finger-
print."

The janitor let them out. Once in the street Krag
put his police whistle to his lips, and a sudden shrill
call rang through the deserted streets.

A few minutes later a couple of policemen came
running up. They were much surprised to find their
Chief there, and at once saw that something unusual
must have happened.

Krag gave them an emphatic order to watch the
house-door, and to let no one out of the house who
did not belong in it, and could not prove who he
was.

"But how are we to know whether they belong
in the house or not?" asked the policemen.

"The janitor can tell you," answered Krag.

"Must I stay here all night?" asked the janitor, much alarmed.

"Certainly! But if you would rather go into the house and lie down, and have them wake you every hour, you can do so."

And turning to the policemen, he said:

"The Chief's orders!" And then he left with the Chief.

By now it was two-thirty P. M. Going along the Drammes Road they met the last stragglers from the cafés. At one corner stood a solitary taxi, and they at once made up their minds to take it.

But at the same time two other men, on the opposite side, headed straight for the same taxi, singing as they came, with the evident intention of taking it themselves.

Both parties met at the taxi both wanted to engage, and there they stood, the chauffeur looking questioningly from one group to the other.

The two strangers seemed to be slightly exhilarated or, rather, one of them was well along in liquor.

He staggered up to Krag, and with many hiccoughs, begged his pardon.

" 'Scuse me," he said. "We'll take . . . taxi! Here firsth . . . y'know!"

"Sit down on the bench over there," Krag answered. "Another one will be along in a minute. And it will do you good to cool off a bit."

"Not . . . t'all! Abs'lutely not! Goin' t'get inter . . . taxi . . . dam . . . insultin' . . . fellar! . . ."

The other man tried to calm him.

Asbjörn Krag unbuttoned his overcoat, and showed the chauffeur his police badge, fastened to the inside of his coat. At once the man jumped down from his seat and opened the door of his taxi for the two police officers.

But at that very moment the drunken man gave Krag another push, muttering:

" 'Scuse me . . . dam . . ."

His companion now led him to the nearest bench, where he broke down completely. The Chief of Police looked around for a patrolman. But Krag checked him.

"We have no time. Besides there are patrolmen enough about. If he kicks up too much of a row one or another will run him in."

And then both drove off at top speed.

When they reached police headquarters the Chief of Police called a criminal detective who knew about the mysterious robberies.

His first question was: "Anything new?" "Not a thing." "Any clue?" "Not one." "Very well, you can go."

On the Chief's desk lay a letter addressed to him. The officer leaving the room pointed to it and said as he went: "It was delivered about ten minutes ago, and they said there would be no answer."

Krag and the Chief were now alone, and hung their overcoats on the wall.

The Chief of Police opened the letter and read it. Then, suddenly, he dropped into a chair. "No, that beats all! . . . " he murmured. "Heavens above!"

Krag hurriedly took the letter from his hand.

It was another sheet of typewritten paper and read:

"Mr. Chief of Police:

Since I can well imagine that we will have more or less correspondence in the future, I should like to make it easy for you always to identify me. On the enclosed blank you will find my finger-print. It is a better and clearer one than that which you took tonight in Bygdö Alley, and for that reason I have taken the liberty of destroying the other. This blank, as you will see, is the same kind used every day in the criminal division at police headquarters.

With sincerest regards,
The Man of the Villa Rosenhain."

Krag started up as though stung by a wasp, and for the first time in years a curse escaped him.

"Compare it!" cried the Chief of Police. "Compare it with the impression on the thumb-tacks!"

Krag felt in his pocket. He searched them feverishly. "They are gone!" he finally said.

"Gone? Impossible! Then you must have forgotten them in Bygdö Alley."

"No."

"Then have you lost them?"

"No," answered Krag, and the man peering in at the kitchen window, who had seen him put the thumb-tacks in his pocket, crossed his mind.

"They have been stolen from me!" Krag declared.

The Chief of Police looked at him. Almost a whole minute long there was silence. Then the Chief of Police burst out laughing. But still Krag did not utter a word.

At last his superior said: "It seems to me, Krag, as though our little investigation were going to take some time. How late is it?"

Krag put his hand to his pocket—then drew it back again.

"My watch is also gone," he said. And a moment later he added: "And my police shield. That is the worst of all."

"Who could have robbed you of all this?"

"You forget the drunken man," answered Krag, and then putting his hand to his forehead, he went on: "I keep forgetting that in this matter I am fight-

ing men who have made a science of crime. But
from now on I shall not forget it."

Although this new occurrence in itself was amusing enough, it did not seem to amuse the Chief of
Police very greatly. The genial smile had left his
face and had yielded to an unusual nervousness.

Asbjörn Krag sat very quietly in his chair and
watched him. "Well, what is your opinion?" he
asked. "Is there any reason for apprehension?"

"I hope that matters will not go on in this way,"
was the Chief's ungracious reply. "I can put up
with being robbed myself, for I am a Police Chief,
and do not concern myself with the detail of investigation. But it seems strange to me that my best
detective, first of all, cannot prevent the pockets of
those at a social gathering where he himself is present, from being picked, and that then he is robbed
in the middle of the street. What would you say
yourself?"

"It is a most mysterious affair," murmured Krag.

The Chief of Police paced restlessly up and down.
"I am surprised that you take the whole affair so
lightly," he replied.

Krag stifled a yawn. "The fact is I am sleepy.
Over-exertion always tires me."

"Then you had better go home and get to bed.
Beginning with tomorrow morning we must turn
over a new leaf in this matter. We are getting

nearer and nearer a public scandal. If twenty-four hours pass without our being able to foil these fellows, it is certain that the papers will get wind of it. And then the whole country will laugh at us. We will never be able to live it down."

Krag nodded.

"No doubt about it," he murmured. "But I think our noble enemies also will have to take a little rest. They have a pretty strenuous day behind them. And tomorrow they have a still more strenuous morning to which to look forward. You remember: they are to meet us at three o'clock in the Continental Hotel."

"I do not believe anything will come of that meeting."

"Why not?"

"Because I do not think the gentlemen in question will turn up."

"I think they will," answered Krag.

The Chief of Police sat down at his desk, to arrange some papers, but in his excitement he disarranged them instead.

"The strangest thing of all," he remarked, "is how these people manage to track us. We must be surrounded by spies."

"No doubt," Krag agreed. "And these spies are extremely efficient. The two drunken men on the Drammes Road were really capital. I think every step we take is watched. And they are not spies who do their work by haphazard. They are working according to a system, a very carefully thought out and cleverly followed plan. It is very alarming."

"Well, and what are we to do?" asked the Chief of Police, as he looked up.

"Our course is clearly indicated," was Krag's answer. "For now, at any rate, we at least have a starting-point for our investigations."

"A starting-point? What do you mean? I must confess that I do not see one. All I see is hopelessness and darkness."

"Then you forget what we have just been discussing," replied Krag, as he rose and began to button his overcoat.

"The spies?"

"Yes, the spies. Until now we did not believe that they would venture to attack us, the police themselves. Such colossal audacity was something with which we did not credit these gentlemen. Yet now they even have had the unexampled impertinence to suggest a conference with us tomorrow in a public restaurant. These people must know that they are putting themselves in serious danger. And that is something they would not do without good reason. They are following some plan in luring us to the Continental tomorrow. That much may be taken for granted. Yet since they are uncertain whether or not we will appear in force, they naturally will continue to watch us. We are in danger of running across all sorts of other tricks of theirs besides those they already have played. Besides the leader, it is evident that some younger hot-heads are members of the gang, ambitious fellows who have imagination, interest and courage. No matter where we may be, we may be sure there will be members of the gang around us, in all sorts of disguises. One may be a policeman, another a street cleaner, one a servant, another a drunken man or a waiter. But the very strength of the gang turns into a weakness, because they have been unable to hide the fact that they *are* tracking us. You must admit that in the long run it will be impossible for them to conceal their spies under continual disguises, once we know who they are."

The logic of these considerations had its effect on the Chief of Police. "I shall keep an eye on them," he said, "but what shall we do if we discover a spy?"

"For the moment we will only be observers. But circumstances may arise that will make it necessary for us to move from defense to attack."

The Chief of Police shook hands with Krag. "Then we meet tomorrow at eight o'clock?"

"At eight o'clock sharp."

"Very well, we will have the whole morning at our disposal."

As Krag went he heard one of the clerks reporting to the Chief: "The newspapers were telephoning us like mad all evening. Strange reports of alleged crimes have been received."

"From whom did they receive the reports?" asked the Chief.

"All were anonymous—telephoned in. The papers ought to know whether there is anything to them."

"Tell the newspapers it is some drunken man's joke. Say that police headquarters have no news of anything out of the way having occurred."

"And nothing has happened?"

"Not a thing."

As Asbjörn Krag entered the vestibule of the house in Bygdö Alley, the officer on duty moved to open the door for him, but Krag begged him not to trouble himself. He went the whole length of the hall, and gradually turned out the lights at the last window of the ground floor which looked out on Young Street. Then, in the darkness, he stationed himself by the window and looked out.

In the deep shadow further down on Möller Street, the detective saw an auto posted as though waiting for some one.

Krag stood watching it for several minutes and then, since it did not move, returned to his post in the vestibule.

"Now you can let me out," he said to the policeman. The officer opened the door and Krag carelessly stepped down the broad flight of stairs, lighting a cigar as he did so.

When he reached the street he took his time before going any further, then turned in the direction of City Hall, slowly and carefully buttoning up his overcoat.

Next he crossed Möller Street in the direction of Carl Johan Street. He had taken only a few steps when he heard an auto drive up behind him. But he did not turn his head, and the auto slowly rolled past. It was a closed public taxi, and the sign "For Hire" was displayed.

As the taxi glided past him the chauffeur slowed up.

Krag knew where he was at once. He called, and the chauffeur stopped quickly and readily. Krag climbed in, gave the chauffeur his address and the taxi drove off.

Through the glass pane Krag took a good look at his driver. He was a young man, hardly more than thirty years of age, and wore a brand-new uniform.

The trip to Krag's home lasted only a few minutes. Krag got out and stepped up beside the chauffeur to pay him. For a minute he pretended to look for his money, watching the driver while he did so. So far as he could see by the dim light, the man was not disguised.

The chauffeur read off the fare: "Ninety *ore!*" said he. "That can't be possible," answered Krag. "Have you a search-light so that we can see what the meter really says?" But no, the driver had no search-light.

Krag paid him with a five-crown note, and the chauffeur had to change it for him. That took a little while. The detective looked about the street. It was empty and deserted. At last the fare was paid, and Krag passed through his house-door after having wished the taxi-driver a curt goodnight.

As soon as Krag had entered the dark hall, he pulled off his overcoat and threw it in a corner.

Meanwhile the taxi-driver was backing up, and his engine made so much noise that he could not tell whether Krag passed on upstairs or remained standing in the hall.

The taxi drove back the same way it had come. As soon as it was in motion, Krag rushed out of the door and "hooked on" behind the speeding machine.

He was as good as a professional acrobat at any trick of the kind, and hung to the taxi as though glued on, completely hidden by the darkness and the shadow the taxi itself threw. In Willow Street several night hawks called out to the taxi-driver, but he paid no attention to them. On the contrary, he stepped on the accelerator.

It seemed as though the drive never would end. First they kept on for a way along the Drammes Road, and finally the taxi, with a sudden jerk, stopped in the neighborhood of Skillebäk.

In his hiding place Asbjörn Krag heard footsteps on the frozen snow then voices became audible and two men entered the auto and it moved off at once.

The chauffeur drove across Monksbridge Way, turned into Meadow Avenue, passed the Tordenskjöld Square, and finally reached the Old Town quarter.

There the taxi stopped before a house in the City Square Street, and its passengers got out, still busily engaged in conversation.

The chauffeur received an order, and drove off again. At the Grand Strand Road Krag jumped off, stood still for a moment, and looked back at the machine. It was turning into Station Square, where it backed into a position among the other taxis parked there.

The number of the taxi was 232.

Krag rang the bell at a Grand Strand Road hotel. He was in a great hurry, and smiled as he murmured to himself: "Things could not be better . . ."

The night porter of the hotel who let Krag in recognized him at once. The detective often took a room in this modest hostelry when he was busy with some case that kept him in the centre of town. Krag always liked to be as near his base of operations as possible, just as when he was resting for the moment he liked to live in the quietest and most peaceful neighborhood he could find.

All he wanted in the hotel this time was to borrow an overcoat. He had been obliged to fling away his own in order to hang on to the auto.

He was given an enormous ulster which some big countryman had forgotten, and when he turned the collar up above his ears, it was quite impossible to recognize him.

First he walked across Station Square to the taxi-stand. There were three taxis parked there, among them the one in which he had ridden. Now the sign once more said "For Hire."

Then Krag returned and went further on into the Old Town quarter. When he was passing the house which the two mysterious night birds had entered, he stopped for a moment to light his pipe.

He used one match after another without being able to get a light. At last there was nothing left for him to do but enter the hallway, where he was protected from the wind. The iron house-door was locked.

As he stood there lighting matches and sucking at his confounded pipe a figure popped up beside him. It was a man in furs, who had come from the street.

Krag stood and cursed his pipe. The newcomer looked him over questioningly, yet with apparent indifference. When he unbuttoned his fur coat to take out his key, Krag noticed that he was in evening dress. He was a man in the thirties, tall, rather muscular and blond.

He unlocked the door, went into the house and disappeared. Krag began to count: first floor . . . second floor. . . . He listened for the footsteps . . . third floor. . . . The steps ceased. So the stranger had gone up to the third story. But who could he have been? Did he live here? What was his business?

Krag went on. When he reached the next taxi station he took a car and drove home.

While still in the street the detective saw a light burning in his room. He smiled. Either my landlady is sick, thought he, or the Chief of Police has some news for me. Well, I shall have some news for him tomorrow morning.

His landlady herself opened the door for him. "Oh," she cried, when she saw him, "now he has gone!"

"Has gone? Who?"

"Yes, he said he did not have time to wait any longer. He left just about half an hour ago."

Krag calmly took off his big ulster and hung it up on a hook in the hall.

"Have I not often told you," he said, "that you never need wait up for me? Do you know what time it is, Mrs. Svendsen? Three-thirty!"

"Yes, but Mr. Holter, the police officer, told me that something very important was under way that needed your attention."

"Was Holter the name the man gave who was here to see me?"

"Yes," said the landlady, hesitatingly. Suddenly she grew quite pale and confused, for it occurred to her that perhaps she had made a mistake again.

"He came from police headquarters and said that it was absolutely necessary for him to speak to you!"

Krag tore open the door to his study and stopped on the threshold. His glance took in the whole room and, so far as he could see, nothing in it had been touched.

Then he turned once more to the landlady. He was entirely self-possessed, and not at all excited. "Of course, you did not let him into my room," he said, "for I have told you time and again never to do it, is that not so?"

"Well, er . . . stammered the landlady as she nervously twiddled her big apron, "he showed me his police shield, and so I took for granted that . . "

Krag smiled. "I understand . . . and I might

as well tell you the man who was here has nothing whatever to do with the police."

"But the shield, the police shield!"

"He had stolen it."

"In the name of all the saints!"

"Goodnight," said Krag, locking himself into his room. First he examined all the drawers and closets. They all were uninjured. Then he unlocked the drawers and went over their contents. He kept everything he had in such excellent order that it was very easy for him to tell that some one had been going through them. But, so far as he could see, nothing was missing. In one drawer he had a few hundred crowns in cash. They still were there. In another drawer he kept two valuable revolvers. They were there. He broke them open: the revolvers were loaded, just as they had been. Nothing was missing.

Krag went to his door and called to the landlady: "How long was he here?"

"One hour," the landlady's frightened voice answered.

Krag calculated that his visitor must have left at about the same time he himself had left police headquarters.

Suddenly an idea struck him. He called once more: "Was the man tall and blonde?"

"Yes," answered the landlady from the outside.

"Was he in evening dress?" "Yes." "In furs?" "Yes."

Then Krag locked the door. No further doubt was possible. The man who had paid him the mysterious visit, and the man who had entered the house in City Square Street were one and the same person.

CHAPTER IV

WHEN THE LAW SCORED

THE next day the Chief of Police waited for some time in vain for any sign of life from Asbjörn Krag. They had agreed to meet at eight o'clock, but Krag did not put in an appearance. On the other hand, his landlady had telephoned a message that the Chief was not to grow impatient, because Krag would turn up in the course of the forenoon.

The Chief, however, grew more and more restless. The clock struck ten, eleven, twelve. The conference in the hotel had been set for three o'clock. At last, when it was nearly one-thirty, Asbjörn Krag appeared. He was wearing sport clothes and was as calm and collected as ever.

"Where have you been keeping yourself?" asked the Chief of Police.

"I was taking a walk," answered Krag. "Nothing more. Is there any news?"

"No, nothing new about our friends of last night." The Chief of Police passed his hand nervously over his face. "This whole affair takes it out of one. It is a distressing groping around in the dark. We know nothing, we cannot even suspect anything. Lis-

ten, Krag, the whole thing seems like a game to
me! Both of us, God knows, are making fools of
ourselves for the benefit of the gang. We are stum-
bling around blindfolded. I did not close an eye
all night!"

"Neither did I," replied Krag.

"I can well imagine it. You lay there and tried
to put the puzzle together, was that it?"

"No, not at all."

"What's that?"

"I took a walk."

"An all-night walk?"

"Yes."

Krag then asked for the reports that had come
in through the day, and the whole bundle was
brought him. They included the usual assaults, petty
larcenies, accidents, fires, etc., but Krag studied them
all with the greatest interest.

The Chief of Police looked at him with astonishment. "What is the matter with you?" he cried.
"Do you think for a minute you will find anything
worth knowing about in the reports?"

Krag did not reply. He looked at his watch, then
leaped from his chair.

"It is time! We are to meet the gentlemen at
three o'clock, you know. I have a taxi waiting
outside."

On the minute of three the two police officers

stepped into the lobby of the Continental Hotel. There the Chief of Police was well known, and as soon as the porter saw him he said, as he opened the elevator door: "I was told to take you gentlemen to a private room as soon as you arrived."

"Who gave you the instructions?" asked Krag.

"The gentleman who is waiting for you, sir."

"Is he already there?"

"Not yet, sir."

"Is he staying at the hotel?"

"No, sir."

The porter took both Krag and his Chief to the second story, where a red-haired waiter bowed and led them through the dining-room to a private cabinet.

The red-headed waiter stopped at the door. "Is there anything the gentlemen want?" he asked. "No, thanks," they said, and off he went.

Once they were alone the Chief of Police looked at Krag and smiled.

"Do you know," he said, "I think this is one of the most curious adventures that ever has happened to me?"

Krag moved over to the window and looked with visible interest at the life in the street below. Before the hotel was a parking place, where four autos were waiting.

Krag suddenly turned around to the Chief of

Police. "No," he said, "I do not think you are right. The whole matter seems pretty clear to me now. It is a section, a part of a complete plan. Nothing more or less. And while we take part in the comedy, we have a chance of being drawn into the plan. And that is all there is to it."

"I have a suspicion that you used your night and forenoon to advantage, after all. I do not believe that you merely went walking for amusement. I believe you went to a number of different places. You seem pretty sure of yourself, like . . ."

* "Like? . . ." asked Krag. He stopped.

"Like a man who had a very poor hand and then suddenly drew a couple of trump cards."

There was a knock at the door. "Come in!"

It was the red-haired waiter. "The gentlemen rang?" he said. "No," was the answer, "we did not ring."

The waiter looked surprised, and was about to leave. But Krag, with a wave of his hand, motioned him to stay. "Listen," he said, "just lock the door!"

The waiter did so. Then Krag, pulling out his watch, said:

"My dear sir, time is passing. What have you to say to us?"

Asbjörn Krag smiled as he said this to the red-haired waiter. "Well," he went on, "don't you think we might as well begin our negotiations?"

The Chief of Police flared up. "With that fellow?" he cried. "With this waiter? Why, I never heard of such a thing!"

"I can assure you," Krag replied, "that he is a very obliging fellow. Just look at his face! It fairly shines with good will and readiness to oblige."

But the red-haired waiter's face glowed only with surprise. At first it was quite unconcealed, but he tried to pull himself together, and after he had flung his napkin into a corner bowed to Asbjörn Krag and said:

"You have anticipated me, my dear sir. I have to admire you!"

"Why do you throw away your napkin?"

"Because I am not a waiter."

"You just asked whether we wanted anything?" Krag continued.

"And you said you did not."

"Quite right. But now we have changed our minds. We want a bottle of soda. Bring us one!"

"You are mistaken. I told you I was no waiter. That is, not now!"

"Hurry up!" Krag took a step toward the push-button. "If you won't serve us we will have to call another waiter. Will you have a seat while we wait for him?"

The detective bowed ironically to the red-haired man and stretched out his hand toward the button.

But with lightning-like swiftness the other man drew a knife.

"Ring if you want to," he said.

"So that's your idea," smiled Krag, while the Chief of Police stepped toward the door.

"Do these fellows mean to lock us in?"

The red-haired man stepped in his way. "No," he said, "you gentlemen are two against one. You have the advantage. You can call the manager and all his waiters, but what will that gain you?"

"That is something we can talk over later on," said the Chief of Police. "We can discuss it in Court, which is the proper place."

"Quite so! Yet since you have taken the trouble to come here to talk to *us* (he emphasized the 'us' in a sarcastic manner), it may be to your interest to listen to what I have to say before you go any further."

The Chief of Police glanced at Krag and the latter nodded. When the red-haired man saw that for the moment, at any rate, he would be heard, he sat down at the table, and invited the others to seat themselves with a movement of his hand.

Krag, as he sat down, laid his watch in front of him, where it was right under his eye, and kept glancing at it as though he expected something definite to happen at a certain time.

The red-haired man, who by now was once more

entirely himself, again looked at Krag with respect. "I will not go so far as to say that you recognized me, for you probably never have seen me before. On the other hand, I will admit that you have a keen eye for detail."

"Allow me to contradict you," Krag answered politely, "but I did recognize you, and that is all there is to it."

"Might I ask when I had the honor of being recognized by you?"

Krag shook his head reproachfully. "Surely we have not come here to discuss such trifles? At this moment it is a matter of entire indifference to me who you are, or how you managed to smuggle yourself into this hotel as a waiter. I assume you are taking the place of one of your international friends. The hotel fairly swarms with foreign waiters. To get down to cases: You wrote us a letter!"

"Yes."

"In that letter you offered to return to the Chief of Police some of the articles you stole from him, did you not?"

"I hereby confirm the offer I made."

With these words the red-haired man pulled out a card-case, and took from it a piece of paper closely covered with writing. "Here," he explained, "is a list of the stolen articles. There were many pretty things among them." And he commenced to read

off the list: "A Venetian glass mirror. Slightly damaged . . ."

The Chief of Police drummed nervously on the
table with his fingers.

"It was in perfect condition," he declared.

The red-haired man interrupted him. "Quite
right. The moving was done very, very quickly.
Besides, we have in our possession . . ."

Angrily the Chief of Police interrupted him: "All
this is unnecessary. You took everything in the
house, bag and baggage."

Again the red-haired man bowed, just like an actor on the stage, and answered: "Quite right. And
what is it that you wish to have returned?"

"Keep all you stole," replied the Chief of Police.
"This is merely a disgusting farce, and I refuse to
have anything further to do with it!"

Asbjörn Krag here interposed. "You must not
misunderstand the Chief," he said. "He means that
either you must return all you have taken or nothing."

"That's asking a good deal," answered the red-
haired man. "I have no instructions on that head."

"Then you yourself are not the thief?"

"Yes, I am one of the thieves."

"But not the leader?"

The red-haired man laughed: "Do you think for
a moment that *he* steals?"

"Who is the brains of your gang, the man who stages all that you do?"

"He never appears in person."

"Then he ought to send some one to represent him who has authority to do so," said Krag. "I can't say that I find this conversation with you very interesting." He gave an order to the waiter, who entered at that moment, and the fellow at once left the room. A few minutes later he returned with bottles and glasses and placed them on the table.

As soon as he had done so, he turned towards the red-haired man with the words: "Allow me!"

As he said this he forced his arms together, and an audible click showed that the red-haired man had been handcuffed. The waiter looked inquiringly at Asbjörn Krag, but the latter merely signalled for him to go.

The Chief of Police and Asbjörn Krag remained with the red-haired man who, strange to say, did not seem the least bit astonished or put out at having been "darbied" so suddenly. He laughed and joked, and even pretended to be very much surprised. "What a misunderstanding!" he cried. "Now your furniture is gone for good, my dear Chief!"

"You might as well give up trying to frighten us," Krag said to him. "Since it is likely that you will be separated from your gang for some time, In fact, you already have been betrayed."

"Is that so?" said the prisoner. "And might I ask when my friends betrayed me? Perhaps when they were drunk the other night in the Drammes Road."

Asbjörn Krag saw the trap and smiled a most amiable smile. "No," he answered, "at that time I knew nothing at all. But I already had made up my mind to accept the invitation to go to the Continental, although I suspected the purpose of the invitation. At nine o'clock this morning I knew your whole plan."

"Then you must have wasted a whole night!"

"I hardly think so, especially if you consider that one of you thieving gentlemen himself carried me home in the gang's own auto."

Both the Chief of Police and Krag could see that this bit of news made an impression on the thief.

"So it will be clear to you," Krag continued, "that I did not waste much time last night sleeping. First, of course, I had to take the taxi back to town again . . . and that meant real exertion, for I had to hang on behind, over the gas-tank. But I put up with the inconvenience because it gave me an insight into your plans and your working methods."

"Into our plans, too, you say?" inquired the prisoner, ironically.

"Your plans, too," answered Krag. "For instance, you can see I was well prepared for you.

And so far as your other plans are concerned, I happen to know, my dear fellow, that you are the one who has been picked for the victim."

"How so?" It was plain that the red-haired man was growing more and more surprised.

"You are to be sacrificed. Do I have to spell it all out for you? By your comrades or, rather, by your fellow-thieves! You have an all-powerful, all-knowing chief and commander. He has planned a fine stroke which is to be 'pulled off' today. His plan is surprisingly impudent in the way it takes things for granted, but for that very reason has a good chance of success. In order that the *coup* be carried out, it was necessary to get the Chief of Police and myself away from police headquarters between three and four o'clock this afternoon. That is why this meeting was arranged. And that is why you were selected as the victim, as the members of the gang who could best be spared. For that reason our meeting is not as interesting as might have been expected."

The red-haired man had listened with increasing astonishment, and now seemed dumbfounded. The expression of his face showed plainly enough that Krag had spoken the truth. "Admitting, for the sake of argument, that you are right," he said, pulling himself together, "you do not know so very much, after all."

"I know a great deal more," answered Krag. "Get away from the door!" suddenly cried the detective. "I don't care to have you rap out any signals here in the hotel! I take for granted that you have been working with several others in the place. But, as you may notice, I have posted some of my men here, too."

Krag now turned to the Chief of Police, and again looking at his watch said: "I think the time is about up. It is four o'clock. If you telephone your office now I think you will hear some good news."

The Chief of Police took up the receiver.

"Ask the man on duty," Krag said, "when you left the building."

"What? That's a strange question to ask him. I left headquarters more than an hour ago."

"Ask him, just the same."

The Chief of Police rang and called up headquarters: "Mr. Evendsen," said he, "did you happen to notice when I left the headquarters building?"

The answer the Chief of Police received must have surprised him greatly. He hung up the receiver.

"What did he say?" smiled Krag.

"He said that I stepped through the door not five minutes ago!"

While this telephoning was going on, and especially when he heard the conversation which ensued, the red-haired man grew decidedly nervous. He shuffled about on his chair, and it was plain he had a great desire to get away. But the most surprised man in the room was the Chief of Police. With his fingers trembling on the receiver he stood with an expression of the greatest and most bitter astonishment on his face.

He glanced at Krag and asked: "Do you want to keep on letting this rascal make fools of us?"

Krag smiled. "I can understand how annoyed you must feel," he answered, "but the situation is not serious. You must admit that there is an element of humor about it."

"But while we sit here guarding this red-haired scoundrel, the probability is that another man is wandering about town disguised as myself. You must admit that it a dangerous thing."

"I will admit it," Krag replied, "but nothing ventured, nothing won."

"Well, since you have ordered something to drink, I suppose we might as well drink it, if we have time."

"Yes, I could stand a bracer of some kind. I have been busy since eight o'clock."

"Eight o'clock yesterday evening?"

"No, eight o'clock yesterday morning, Chief. A little refreshment will set me up. And very likely our friend here could stand something as well. From what I can make out he did not sleep well last night."

"What makes you think that?" asked the red-haired man.

"You could not have gone to bed before four o'clock this morning," Krag answered.

"Well you have just about guessed it."

"I never guess."

"But how could you know?"

"I regret that you have such a poor memory. Have you no recollection of my riding with you last night?"

The red-haired man looked at him with astonishment. Krag went on:

"Any one who means to disguise himself, and has hair so peculiar in color as you have should first of all see that it is thoroughly hidden. It is a very peculiar shade of red. It was not enough merely to slap a dark wig over it. You trusted too much to the darkness—but in spite of the dark I saw your red hair in the light of the taxi lamp!"

"Well, perhaps you are telling the truth, but I hope you will admit I am a good driver."

"You are a first-class driver. And above all, you were discreet."

"What do you mean by that? Didn't I take you home and drive off without spying on you?"

"Quite true. And you drove off without making sure that you had no one hitching on behind your car. That was very tactful."

The red-haired man muttered a curse. Krag soothed him. "Don't forget that strangers may hear you? We must not make any noise in this room, otherwise we may be disturbed."

There was a knock at the door. A waiter came in with bottles of seltzer water and the red-haired man lowered his head so that his colleague would not see him.

The waiter poured. Krag gave the Chief of Police a signal and both took up their glasses. The red-haired man hesitated. The waiter had remained standing behind his chair after he had loosened his handcuffs.

"I'm not thirsty," said the red-haired man.

"Well, you will have to drink whether you are or not," answered Krag. "There is no use in being impolite."

"Very well," said the red-haired man, with a sly smile, "then I will drink with you." He raised his glass and sniffed at it, then set it down again.

"May I have another glass?"

"Certainly," answered the waiter. He went to the door, but the red-haired man held him back.

"Thanks, but you need not go so far. Let me have the glass over there!" He pointed to a glass which stood alone by the water-cooler. "That one will do nicely!"

The waiter's eye crossed those of Krag, and the detective's face twitched in a hardly noticeable manner.

Then the waiter brought the desired glass. The red-haired man smiled like a person who has gained his point, poured seltzer-water into his glass and drank.

But after the first swallow he looked frightened. Then he threw the glass on the floor.

"Poisoners!" he cried.

With that he rose violently from his chair. But he was at once folded in the "waiter's" giant arms, and before he knew it had once more been handcuffed. Both Krag and the Chief quietly kept their places.

In a few seconds the red-haired man's struggles ceased, and suddenly he slumped down in his seat and slid to the floor like a damp cloth. He remained lying on the carpet. His eyes were closed, but his mouth was wide open, and he breathed heavily.

Krag bent over him. "That will keep him quiet for half a day," he murmured, and turning to the "waiter," he continued: "You are a first-class parlor magician, Ivan, and you certainly got the sleeping powder into the glass like a professional."

Krag poured out the rest of the seltzer water.

"We cannot run the risk of more of us falling asleep," he said. Then, turning to the Chief of Police, he added: "Well, now the line is clear! For the first time we have scored a success!"

"All I can see is that we have made this fellow unconscious for the time being. And that is not very much."

"You forget that the man has accomplices here in the hotel. It was his business to detain us here or elsewhere as long as possible, while his more daring comrades carried out some stroke. And if things went wrong, it was his duty to warn his friends that danger threatened.

Krag looked questionably at the "waiter"—who was none other than the herculean police officer Jarven—and pointed to the walls.

"Both occupied," answered Jarven. "I have a "couple" in the one room and, well I guess you can hear what is going on in the other."

"Yes, some one is tuning the piano."

"Just so. It is Oppen."

"I did not know he was musical."

"He's not, sir!"

"Well, the piano is going to get a fine tuning then."

"First-class!"

"Naturally," said Krag to the Chief, "I have seen to it that some of our men were close at hand. One of the adjoining rooms is occupied by the "couple," the other by a piano-tuner whose musical or, rather, unmusical offerings will prevent any eavesdropping. And with all this we have secured the following results: first our "Carrot" has been put completely out of commission, at least for a few hours. Furthermore, he has been given the quietus so silently that no one could have noticed it. We easily can hide the fact that he is helpless for another half hour. That will be enough. Jarven will stay here in order to lead the red-haired rascal's friends astray."

"And what do we do now?" asked the Chief of Police.

"We start out to meet the Chief of Police of Christiania, and the well-known if not always successful detective Asbjörn Krag."

"Have we both doubles?"

"Yes, indeed."

Krag went to the telephone and took a message from the police headquarters. When he heard it he said: "Our doubles left headquarters about twenty minutes ago. Not a minute later. They were accompanied by a gentleman who spoke some foreign language, and who had come to headquarters and asked for the Chief of Police."

"And the false Chief of Police was sitting in my office at the time?"

"Yes."

"And then they went out together?"

"Yes, the Chief of Police, Asbjörn Krag and the foreigner," said the detective, laughing.

"But suppose the foreign gentleman has hunted me up with regard to some matter of real importance, what then? Why, there is no telling what the consequences might be!"

"Nothing of the kind."

"Why not?"

"You forget," Krag explained, "that I did not sleep last night, but was busy every minute of the time."

"I don't understand . . ."

"You will see the whole thing when I tell you that our doubles at the present moment are at the Grand Hotel, in Room No. 26. It is the so-called 'Royal Suite.' If we drive straight over there, we can make the acquaintance of these interesting gentlemen, and find out what we really look like. You may rely upon it that the disguises are first class."

"The auto is waiting!" reported Jarven.

"It is high time for us to start," said Krag, buttoning his gloves.

"I don't believe in hurrying. But unnecessary delay may cost us more now than the most reckless haste. I think that in four or five minutes the psychological moment will have arrived."

And nodding to the Chief of Police, he added, "It is possible that a revolver may come in handy."

"I have one," said the Chief.

"Good!"

"But what are we to do with that fellow?" queried the Chief, pointing to the red-haired man.

"We will ask a couple of his comrades to look out for him," answered Krag. The two officers disguised as waiters standing close by understood what he meant and smiled.

As the Chief and his companion passed through the hall, the former said: "What seems most surprising of all is that you have men posted everywhere, though yesterday, when we parted, you were dead set against it."

"That's true," answered Krag, as he opened the door of the dining-room for the Chief. "When we parted yesterday, I was of that opinion. Only new developments could have induced me to change my mind. And those developments occurred last night."

"So that's it! And that is why you could not manage to get to sleep last night?"

"Yes, that was why."

The great dining-room of the Continental Hotel was only half full. The echoes of the latest sentimental waltz floated softly from the musicians' platform, and died away across the snowy tables. The waiters circulated noiselessly over the soft carpet.

All breathed peace and comfortable ease, with only the popping of a champagne-cork in one corner to lend life to the scene.   And so the human comedy went on, with actors presenting different scenes within the walls that separated one room from the other.   .

As Krag walked through the dining-room with the Chief of Police he suddenly said in a loud tone of voice, so that those at the tables could hear him: "Well, that certainly was a curious experience!"

The Chief of Police started at him without any idea of what he meant.

"Yes, indeed, it was very strange," he murmured, hesitatingly.

"I think we shall have to return to your home," Krag went on.

"Yes, that would probably be the best thing to do," the Chief said, for now he began to catch Krag's drift.

When they reached the cloak-room the Chief asked:

"Was any one there?"

"Did you see the man with the dark beard and gold-rimmed eye-glasses who was sitting at the left, under the big picture?"

"Yes, I saw him."

"Good, that's the man!"

"Who is he?"

"One of the members of the gang."

"What are we to do with him?"

"Let him sit there. He heard what we were saying, and it probably reassured him. He does not suspect what has happened in our private room."

"What makes you think so?"

"Because all the red-haired waiter had to do was to hold us here in conversation, and then to disappear. The man with the gold-rimmed glasses thinks the red-haired scamp has carried out his instructions. That is all."

As they slipped on their overcoats Krag said: "I hope my proposal did not surprise you?"

"For a moment I was surprised, but I saw at once the situation had changed."

Krag nodded in reply and both went down the steps together.

The hotel-porter accompanied them to the auto and opened the door.

"Bygdöo Alley No. 44," said Krag to the chauffeur. Then both he and the Chief got in.

As soon as the auto had started the Chief of Police said: "Now I *am* surprised! Are we really going to my house?"

"No," was Krag's answer, "we are just going a little ways in that direction."

When the car had nearly reached the Drammes Road, Krag knocked at the window and called out to the chauffeur: "Drive us to the Grand Hotel!"

"Nothing but precautionary measures," growled the Chief of Police. "Did you suspect the man who opened the door for us?"

"One never can be too careful," said Krag, "at least not when one is playing the game with opponents like ours. We are in the middle of the enemy's camp. In fact, we are marching straight up to his "artillery.""

The auto stopped in front of the Grand Hotel. Asbjörn Krag nodded to the porter, who knew him. The latter seemed somewhat surprised to see the detective. In the hotel lobby Krag stepped up to the room-chart and studied it for a moment.

"I think we are not too late, after all," he then whispered to the Chief of Police. "They are on the third floor. We had better use the stairs."

On the way up nothing unusual occurred, but when they reached the third floor and were walking along the long, carpeted corridor, the Chief of Police had an experience he never yet had made in the course of his whole official life.

He met—himself!

We will have to make this a little clearer. The Chief of Police and Asbjörn Krag were not in uniform: both were wearing summer suits. Krag had on a light brown overcoat, a brown business suit, black derby and gray gloves; the Chief of Police a light overcoat, morning coat, a Fedora hat, and was holding his gloves in his hand. And the two gentlemen whom they now met in the corridor were dressed exactly like them. One wore a light overcoat, morning coat and a soft Fedora hat, and was carrying his gloves; the other had on a brown overcoat, business suit and black derby, and wore gray gloves. It seemed to the Chief of Police and to Krag that they were standing before a looking-glass, and that both their doubles drew near them as a reflection walks forward to meet one in a mirror.

And the doubles did not alone resemble their models in their dress. They resembled them in appearance as well. They had the same faces, the same beards, the same walks.

And not only did they agree with them in their external appearances, but it seemed as though these doubles were the very same beings as the Chief and the detective, within as well as without.

Both parties seemed to be equally astonished at meeting each other.

After they had mechanically taken a few extra steps all stood still.

It was too ludicrous!

The Chief of Police put his hand to his forehead as though to brush away a ghost. And the human reflection of himself which stood opposite him did the same.

Then the Chief of Police uttered an exclamation, while Krag said: "These are the men!"

And as he noticed that one of the men—the man who represented him—put his hand into his pocket, he promptly followed his example.

Then the man opposite him smiled, and said in excellent Norwegian, but with a slight yet unmistakeable accent: "Among civilized people the custom of giving one a chance to explain one's self always should be observed."

"That is my intention," answered Krag, "but you will have to admit, gentlemen, that in this particular case *we* are the ones who are entitled to the explanation."

"Certainly. Does this corridor seem well suited for such a conference?"

"It is a matter of indifference to us where we confer."

"There is a drawing-room here at the right," Krag's double remarked, "suppose we go in there."

"Gladly! I shall ask you gentlemen to step in first."

The two strangers nodded to each other, and then slowly walked back along the corridor. The two others followed. When the strangers reached the door of No. 12, Krag's double, who evidently was the leader, said: "But here the laws of hospitality compel us to ask you gentlemen to step in first!"

He opened the door.

"Not at all," was Krag's reply. "We are meeting by chance in a hotel. There is neither host nor guest."

The stranger bowed. "But won't you gentlemen honor us by taking precedence, in spite of the fact?"

"Thanks," replied Krag. "But then we should be running the risk of having the door slammed on us as soon as we were inside."

"Since you are suspicious," returned the stranger, "I see no other way out of it. We will have to go in first ourselves."

"We cannot agree to that, either."

"Then we shall have to remain out here in the corridor."

"No."

Both strangers smiled. How extremely polite they looked, both of them standing there, half-leaning forward to bow.

"Then we must leave it for you to decide what we are to do," said the one and nodded to Krag. "It almost seems as though we were confronted by a riddle we cannot solve."

"Not at all," said Krag. "I will ask my friend to enter the room first."

The Chief of Police understood, and went to the door.

"It is quite in order," remarked the second

stranger, "for the Chief of Police to take first place."

The real Chief entered the room, at once drew down the shades, and turned on the light. It was a large drawing-room with a fire-place. All three windows looked out on Karl Johann Street.

"And now," continued Asbjörn Krag, "the rest of the problem is very easily solved. The gentleman who represents the Chief of Police will be the next to enter the room."

"Ah, yes, I understand," said the gentleman in question, "we enter in order of rank."

So the first stranger followed the real Chief. Krag and the man who was impersonating him now remained.

"By rights it is your turn now," said the latter.

"This is where we break the regular order," declared Krag.

"Very well, then in I go." The stranger entered the room and Krag at once followed him.

The moment Krag entered he shut the door, then pushed the electric call-button.

The two strangers stood by the fire-place.

"Suppose we all sit down," suggested Krag.

"Should we not first make each other's acquaintance?" asked the man who seemed to be the leader.

"You are well acquainted with us," answered Krag, "but we haven't the honor of knowing you."

"My name is Ferro," replied the stranger. "And this gentleman is my friend Mr. Raspail. I am an Italian and my friend is French. He does not speak Norwegian very well, but he understands every word we are saying."

The Frenchman smiled.

"Yes, yes," he answered. "I understand." ·

"Permit us to take off our overcoats," Ferro went on, and without waiting for Krag's permission he laid down his overcoat and hat, and his friend did the same. The Norwegians followed his example. There the four gentlemen stood and looked at each other. It was a very comical situation, for both strangers still seemed the very image of the men they were impersonating.

"Do you care to take off anything else?" asked Krag. "Your false wig and beard, for instance?"

But the Italian shook his head decidedly.

Then all four sat down. At that moment there was a knock at the door.

"Ah, you rang!" said the Italian. "Perhaps you are going to ask us to have something to drink."

The waiter stood in the doorway.

"Push the call-bell," Krag said to him. The waiter looked at him blankly.

"Ring the bell and stay where you are."

The waiter did as he was told. At once a second waiter appeared.

"Fetch the porter!" Krag told him.

The latter came. Krag wrote a few words on a sheet of paper and sent him off with it.

The Italian inquired: "What does this mean? Are you arresting us?"

"Of course, I am arresting you." Krag pointed to the waiter: "We are now three to one, so resistance would be useless.'

"I understand that. And we are not making any trouble, though we are armed. Do you want us to give up our arms?"

The stranger put his hand in his pocket. But Krag waved away his offer.

"No, thanks," said he, "it is not necessary. You may keep your arms."

The Italian smiled slyly.

"You are very careful, but not very bright."

"How so?"

"If you were as bright as I gave you credit for being, you would have known long ago that if we had intended to use revolvers we would have done so at the very start. For then we had the best chance."

"I take for granted that you acted wisely," Krag remarked. "You must have known that we had our men posted near by."

"A good deal can be accomplished with two revolvers. The Norwegians are not used to such fare. If we did not use our revolvers it was because we had a definite reason not to do so."

"Might one ask what your reason was?"

"There is no objection at all. The reason I did not shoot was because I decided shooting was unwise. I felt it would be an advantage not to pull our guns."

"You were absolutely right," Krag answered. "You would have made your case much worse if you had added a murder or attempted homicide to your other crimes."

The Italian cut a wry face. "You misunderstand us," he said.

Krag smiled. "I do not misunderstand you for a single moment. I am only acting as though I did. Incidentally, let me thank you for the compliment you have paid me."

The Italian slowly bent his head, as though *he* were expressing his thanks.

Then he asked: "Of what are we accused?"

"Of a series of extremely impudent robberies. I have the honor"—the detective rose from his chair —"of standing in the presence of the man who meant to plunder Christiania."

The Italian smiled: "Very flattering," said he, "but can you prove it?"

"It can be proved."

"Very well. And of what else are we accused?"

"Of a very unique kind of imposture."

Krag waved his hand at the strangers. "Need I go into details? Don't your disguises speak for themselves?"

"That may be a practical joke."

"It is a very serious joke."

"Have you any evidence?"

"Not yet," replied Krag, "but I can get it at a minute's notice."

To the men standing in the door he said:

"Ask the gentleman in Room 26 to come here."

The Italian made a movement.

When the waiter heard the order he hesitated. "Is the gentleman in Room 26 the one you want?"

"Yes," replied Krag.

"Then I ought to tell you," said the waiter, "that No. 26 is the royal suite."

"I know that."

"The millionaire James Vanderock has taken it."

"We are losing time," remarked Krag. "Just be good enough to ask the gentleman in Room 26 to come to this room. Excuse yourself, and tell him the message comes from police!"

The waiter disappeared. When he had gone the Italian remarked: "I admire you in spite of all. You must know more about things than we thought you did."

"Then you admit," said Krag, smiling, "that I am

on the right track when I want to speak to the gentleman in Room 26."

"Perhaps," answered the Italian, "let us wait and see."

"You have disguised yourself as Asbjörn Krag," the detective continued. "I regard it as a compliment that the leader of this notorious gang has preferred to appear in my likeness."

At that moment heavy footsteps were audible outside. Some one knocked at the door and in stepped two men. They were the police "waiters" from the Continental Hotel.

They looked at the two pair of doubles sitting opposite each other with surprise.

Krag pointed to the two strangers. "Those are the counterfeits," said he, "we two are genuine."

"We understand," replied one of the police officers, smiling. "We are gradually getting used to disguises."

"Arrest those two men," Krag went on. "Since it is quite possible that we will be unable to accompany you, you must be on your guard. Don't take your eyes off them!"

"You may rely on us. We'll not let them give us the slip. We just took the red-haired fellow to the station-house. He is wide awake now and furious."

"I can imagine he would be," said Krag. And

pointing to the Italian he added: "That fellow is
the dangerous one, the leader of the gang!"

"Good!"

"Both of them are armed. I guess you had better
relieve them of their weapons."

The police officers went through the pockets of
the two men and found that each had a Browning
revolver in his possession.

"Have you handcuffs?"

"Right here!"

"We will need them later."

Turning to his opponents Krag remarked: "I
might as well inform you that the least attempt at
resistance will be made at your own risk, gentlemen.
Above all, we do not intend to give you a chance to
get away. I'll not pretend that this is not a threat.
you understand?"

The Italian nodded his head affirmatively.

"And your friend? Does he understand as well?"

"*Merci,* thank you," replied the Frenchman, "I
understand all you say."

Now a tall portly gentleman entered the room.
He might have been anywhere from fifty to sixty
years of age. His hair was white, his face red and
weather-beaten, full of prominent veins. It would
have been almost a repelling face had it not been
for the eyes, which were bright with intelligence and
good humor. Those keen eyes gave the entire face

an unusual amount of vitality. Any one who had seen them could not help but look at their owner a second time.

The gentleman wore an everyday, dark brown traveling suit. He held his hat in his hand. Besides the waiter he was accompanied by a tall dark young man armed with a camera, evidently his secretary. The American stepped into the room and bowed in a questioning manner. As he did so, at a signal from from Krag, the waiter shut the door quietly behind him.

Krag rose and stepped up to the American.

"Mr. James Vanderock?" he said in English. "You know me and I know you. Take a good look at me!"

The American straightened up at this mode of address. Then he examined the detective from head to foot.

Next he turned to the two disguised suspects sitting by the fire-place. At once a merry twinkle appeared in his eyes.

"First rate," he said in English. "I understand in part, but not everything."

Then he turned to his secretary and continued: "Mr. Gibson, that's a picture we simply must have!"

The secretary nodded and promptly focussed his camera.

"It's too bad," murmured Mr. Vanderock, "that

the gentlemen are not in uniform. That would have been a treat for my friends on the other side."

He turned to Asbjörn Krag and said: "My time is valuable, but I am entirely at your disposal for five minutes."

"It is quite possible that I will not have to take even that much of your time," Krag answered. "I merely wish to verify a few facts. These two gentlemen visited you a short time ago, did they not?"

"Not exactly," replied the millionaire. "It was I who first paid these two gentlemen a visit."

Krag nodded. "But it was at their request."

"Absolutely."

The millionaire turned to his secretary. "This is my confidential secretary. Mr. Gibson has the papers. Show him the curious letter."

Krag waved it away. "That is not necessary for the moment. I know that you arrived in Christiania yesterday, and that you received a letter on the official paper of the police department, asking you to come to the office of the Chief of Police for a conference."

The American nodded affiratively. "Yes, I went there at three o'clock."

"Did you know in advance what the conference was to be about?"

"The letter contained a hint that it was a matter of the greatest interest to me. Otherwise I should have not gone there, of course. My time is precious."

Once more the American glanced at his watch. His secretary, meanwhile, had taken his snapshot.

Krag went on with his examination: "And when you entered the police department building you were shown into the office of the Chief of Police. There you met the two gentlemen sitting on the other side of the room?"

Krag pointed to the two imposters.

Again the American agreed with him. "It might just as well have been yourself, my dear sir," he said. "Though now I see that it was the two gentlemen yonder."

The two imposters smiled at one another.

"And when you had greeted each other," Krag went on, "the proposal was made to go to your room in the Grand Hotel in order to continue the conference undisturbed."

"Quite right."

"Did your negotiations lead anywhere?"

"No, the two gentlemen were to return in the course of the afternoon."

"To conclude the negotiations?"

"That is not exactly the right expression," said the American. "It would be more correct to say that we had concluded our discussion of one certain point."

Asbjörn Krag nodded eagerly, as though he knew exactly what the other man meant.

"May I ask the nature of these negotiations?"

"You may ask, certainly, but I am not inclined to answer you here and now. I will only say it was a question of certain measures of safety which were to be taken."

"But now you know that you had fallen into the hands of two clever and impudent deceivers?"

"Yes." The American looked around. "Yes," he repeated. "You must be the genuine ones and the others over there in the corner the false ones."

The porter came to Krag's assistance. "There can be no question about it," he said. "I know these gentlemen."

"Hence the information that the fraud has been discovered is good news for you," Krag went on, quite undisturbed.

"I am very much obliged."

"Of course, various plans were under consideration in connection with this attempted fraud."

"Quite right. Two persons do not expose themselves to serious danger without a reason."

"Let us take for granted that the imposters had been successful. Their object would have been to secure a sum of money, would it not?"

"Yes, it was a question of money."

"Might I ask how large a sum was involved?"

"It was not a question of a sum of money, but of a fortune. I was to be protected against a danger which threatened me."

The American pointed to the two impostors: "They offered to protect me. So you can form your own opinion."

"You used the word 'fortune.' Do you mean a fortune in the Norwegian or in the American sense of the word?"

Mr. James Vanderock was silent for a moment. He was calculating.

"In the American sense," he then replied.

Those present started. But the American was evidently growing impatient. In order to quiet him Asbjörn Krag now looked at his watch.

"One last question," said the detective. "Was the danger against which these two rascals were to protect you a real or an imaginary one?"

"A real one."

"And it still exists?"

"Yes."

"Here in Christiania?"

"Yes."

"Thanks. Then I have no further questions to ask of you. Your five minutes are just up."

The American retired, accompanied by his secretary. Krag felt that he had not spoken to Vanderock for the last time that day.

Now it was the turn of the two swindlers. They were to be taken to police headquarters for examination.

In spite of the crowd of persons involved, police officials, guests, porters and waiters, apparently the whole affair had gone off without attracting attention.

That was due first of all to the prisoners themselves. Asbjörn Krag was obliged to admit to himself that the peaceful, almost smiling confidence of the two criminals made him feel a little out of countenance. They had not made the slightest attempt to escape. They had been taken by surprise, and had resigned themselves to their fate as though they were as innocent as new-born babes—and yet they had quietly and confidently admitted their crimes. Did they have something up their sleeves?

Before Krag gave the signal to start, he mustered the assembly. Besides Krag and the Chief of Police there remained the two criminals, the two police officers, the waiters and the porter. It was quite a little crowd and almost filled the small drawing-room.

Krag turned to the criminals. "You will have no objection, I hope," said he, "to our taking the usual precautions?"

"What do you mean?" replied the Italian.

"We shall have to put you in irons."

The impostor looked uncomfortable. "Then you are not going to jail with us?"

"No," replied Krag. "I have something else to attend to at the moment."

"And so you send handcuffs instead! You are not very romantic by nature. Since you insist on regarding me as the master criminal, the dangerous and skilful leader of the gang"—with that the Italian smiled—"I cannot object to being treated like a street robber. But I can assure you that my companion really is an old man."

The "old man" whose name was Raspail, had finally grown quite silent and uninterested in the proceedings. He did not even appear to hear what was said. Krag looked at him and was struck by his slender white hands in which a network of thin blue veins stood out. He did not put much faith in the age which showed in his face, but those hands could not lie. He really was an old man; one of the Italian's poor, weak tools. A man who shambled along after his leader, with no initiative of his own. So Krag decided to dispense with the handcuffs in his case. It was quite plain that the man did not realize what was going on about him—he appeared altogether indifferent. On the other hand a gleam of recognition showed in the younger criminal's eyes. He made it easy for the officers to handcuff him. The iron bracelets were hidden by his coat sleeves.

CHAPTER V

FOOLED AGAIN

ASBJORN KRAG remained in the hotel with the Chief of Police, while the officers led away the two imposters whom they had arrested. The arrest had attracted no attention. The handcuffs were not visible, and the constant stream of people passing in and out of the hotel deprived the egress of the quartet of any element of the unusual.

Asbjörn Krag led the Chief of Police a story higher, and there hunted up the millionaire in Room 26. Vanderock was busy dictating a letter to his secretary at the moment. Yet when he heard who wished to see him both gentlemen were at once admitted.

"I suspected that you would come to see me," he said very amiably, as he shook hands with them. "There is one point in this affair, however, about which you have not as yet been fully informed. You do not know why I entered into a deal with the two impostors who by this time I hope are safely locked up."

"You consented to deal with them because they pretended to be police officials," replied Krag.

"Otherwise, I am sure you would not have been willing to confide in them."

"Still, that does not fully explain the matter. As I mentioned, the rascals sent me a letter. Well and good. In this letter they threw out certain hints which I could not well afford to ignore. I was simply driven to go to the police station because I was *afraid!* That is an actual fact, whether you believe me or not."

Asbjörn Krag looked at the giant figure of this well-built man, clearly enjoying the best of good health, and smiled as he shook his head with evident disbelief: "Afraid?" he said. "That sound incredible!"

"It is by no means as incredible as you seem to think. You may not know it, but I am a man who has been condemned to death."

"Condemned to death by whom?"

"By a band of murderers!"

"Yes? And why?"

"That is something hard to explain to you. Many things happen in America which would appear quite fantastic and impossible to a European. For instance, we have a band of blackmailers of a kind unknown on your side of the Atlantic. They begin work in the following manner: a rich man receives a letter in which he is told to pay them a certain sum by a certain fixed date. If not, his summer resi-

dence will be burned to the ground. Either he pays
no attention to the letter and leaves the matter to
the police to handle, or else he takes the threat seriously and tries to protect himself. And the whole
thing ends, as a rule, with his summer home being
burned down unless he pays, in spite of all precautions taken.

"But that is only a beginning. It is a comparatively innocent beginning. The next time some
valuable work of art, a fine yacht, or something of
that sort is threatened with destruction. And in the
event the man threatened still refuses to pay, in due
course of time the matter ends in the same way. Yet
if he does pay he does not rid himself of the black-
mailer. The latter grants his victim an extension of
time, and then writes again. And one day he receives the horrible communication: your wife's life
is in danger!

"This is usually the signal for a terrible persecution. In most cases, as I have mentioned, the
blackmailing scheme has taken the course already
described. The scoundrels work according to a carefully considered plan. They show that they fear
nothing, and are capable of any crime. No matter
how powerful, influential or self-confident one may
be, it is out of the question to disregard such a
threat. Many wealthy Americans would be the first
to deny that they pay this blackmail levied on them,

but when they do they are not telling the truth. It is easy to see by their fearless, unconcerned manner that they have paid and thus, so to speak, have insured their lives. The man who would dare revolt against this mysterious tyranny is hunted down with greater cruelty than some wild beast. He knows neither peace nor rest. He lives a life of terror. Continually surrounded by detectives, who guard him with the utmost vigilance, he is still continually obsessed by the fearful thought that all the care of the men he has hired may be powerless to protect him at some given moment. For he knows that he can be destroyed quite as easily as his belongings. Hence it is not surprising that most rich men prefer to submit to the humiliation of quietly paying the tribute demanded. If the threat is ignored the man in question leads a dog's life. His health is soon undermined. His business interests suffer in consequence, and not everyone can immure himself behind the fortress walls of a great estate, regularly patrolled by guards and private detectives.

"And still, in spite of all this, here and there you will find a man who defies the scoundrels. As long as my wife was exposed to the revenge of these criminals, I preferred to pay the blackmail they asked. But when my wife died—of natural causes, of course—and a few months later I was informed that I would be killed unless I paid down $200,000 at

a certain specified place at a certain specified date, I
made up my mind to fight. It was a very interesting
struggle, a kind of relaxation for me! I knew that
the murderers could reach me almost anywhere, and
yet I believed I had a better chance of surviving outside the United States. For that reason I have been
traveling abroad for the past few years. When I
reached your beautiful, peaceful country, I felt distinctly relieved. For a long time I had received no
word from my enemies. And then, quite unexpect-
edly, came the letter from the Chief of Police. The
letter was a forgery, but of course, I could not know
that. In the letter the struggle against my mysterious antagonists was mentioned. I was informed
that a suspicious character who evidently had de-
signs on my life, had been arrested. Enough to say,
I hurried to police headquarters and—the rest you
know. So you must admit that my visit was
prompted by fear!"

"Or by caution," said Krag.

The American shrugged his shoulders.

"But now both of them have been arrested," he
said, "so I presume they will let me alone for a
while!"

"But there are others in the gang besides the two
men."

The American nodded his head. "That is true,"
he said. Then he suddenly added: "I can give you

one bit of information, by the way. The older of the two men, the fellow who looks so despondent . . ."

"You mean Raspail, the Frenchman . . ."

"He is no Frenchman."   ·

"No?"

"He is a Norwegian."

This disclosure was so unexpected that even a man as self-controlled as Krag could not conceal his surprise. And the Chief of Police showed his surprise quite plainly.

"A Norwegian!" he cried. "But in that case we have once more been deceived!"

"Deceived?" said the millionaire, and he frowned. "Gentlemen, you make me uneasy. I hope you have not released the old fellow!"

He moved toward the door, as though he meant to hurry from the room in order to correct the mistake he seemed to think had been made. His secretary let his fingers rest on the keys of his typewriter, and listened with the greatest interest to what was being said.

Krag rang for a bell-boy. Since the millionaire occupied the royal suite, the bell-boys swarmed around his door like flies. At Krag's ring one of them appeared. Krag asked him to find out whether the four gentlemen, the two criminals and the two police officers, already had left the hotel. The answer was that they had driven off in an auto. One man had worn handcuffs, the old, grey-bearded gentleman had not been handcuffed, however, when they had led him into the auto.

It was plain that this news somewhat disquieted Krag: "Are you sure that he was about to faint?" he asked.

"That is what the porter said. They had to support him, and he seemed to have a cramp or something, for he held his hand to his heart."

"Did they leave in a closed car?"

"Yes, that is to say . . ."

"That is to say? . . ."

"It was open, first off. But seeing that the old man was sick, and because they had drawn a crowd, the officers closed the car."

"And all this happened just now?"

"Yes, just a minute or so ago. It was all of ten minutes before they could drive off."

"Very well! And now fetch me a 'phone. But be quick about it!"

A moment later the bell-boy brought a telephone into the room, put it down on the table, and connected it with the wall-plug.

Krag called up police headquarters. "I am expecting a car with two arrested men," he said. "Has it arrived?"

He waited tensely.

"No," was the answer. "No one has been brought in here for the past hour."

Then Krag asked a strange question of the man at the other end of the line. He said: "Where are you now?"

The man to whom he was talking at once caught his meaning. He answered: "I am in booth No. 3."

"You can see the street from where you are standing, can't you?"

"Certainly."

"Good! Take a look at the street, and tell me whether you see a closed auto headed for the building."

"No."

"Then stay where you are at the 'phone, and keep an eye on the street. I will be back again in a minute."

Krag laid down the receiver and turned to the millionaire, who had been listening with apparent indifference in the comfortable leather chair in which he had seated himself.

"I hope you will excuse my taking up your time and your room in so unceremonious a way," Krag said. "But there are a few things I must be certain about just as soon as possible. The fact that you tell me the older gentleman is Norwegian has materially altered matters. How did you know he was a Norwegian, by the way?"

"I do not understand much Norwegian myself,"
answered the millionaire, "but I can tell when any
one is speaking Norwegian without difficulty."

"And you heard the Frenchman who calls himself
Raspail speak Norwegian?"

"Yes, several times. He spoke Norwegian to the
chauffeur who took us here from police headquarters. And he also dropped a few Norwegian words
to the policeman on guard in the hotel vestibule, who
in the darkness must have thought the Chief of
Police himself was talking to him. But at the same
time I must admit that he spoke faultless French as
well. I am a pretty fair French scholar and know."

Asbjorn Krag did not know. He merely signalled
the bell-boy and told him to order an auto for him
at once. Then he again returned to the telephone.

"Hello," he called, "are you still there?"

A voice answered "Yes."

"No auto has turned up yet?"

"No."

Krag pulled out his watch and nervously looked
at the second-hand, which moved along at a snail's
pace.

"The auto should be there," he murmured.
"Either there has been an accident or . . ."

"Or?" queried the Chief of Police, uneasily.

"Or we should have gone along," answered Krag.

"But you are forgetting that there were two

strong-arm men in charge of them," said the Chief
of Police, "and that one of the criminals was handcuffed and the other a sick, old man . . . even
though he was a Norwegian!"

"I do not believe he was sick," remarked Krag.
"In fact, we never should have believed him to be
sick . . .Hello!"

"The voice at the other end of the telephone was
speaking again: "Now I see the auto! It is a closed
yellow car and is coming along Moller Street."

"Correct."

"But it is driving very slowly."

"That explains why it is so late."

"Now it is stopping in front of headquarters."

"Be sure you notice exactly who gets out," said
Krag eagerly.

There was a pause.

"The auto has stopped," the voice said, after a
time, "but no one is getting out of it!"

"Look carefully! Be sure you see who gets out
of it!" Krag called.

Again there was a pause. And then Krag heard
a voice say: "No one is getting out of the auto at
all. And the chauffeur is looking around as though
surprised. It is all very strange!"

"Can't you see whether there is any one in the
auto?" Krag asked.

"No," replied the voice, "but it does not seem to

be empty. It seems to me as though there were figures in it. But they are sitting quite still . . . Ah, now the chauffeur is getting down! Now he is going to open the door. But he is hesitating . . . He seems to be frightened at something. He is looking around. He is coming into the station-house. He is entering the door! . . ."

Krag hastily said, in the most urgent and pre-emptory manner:

"Run down at once and see what the trouble is! Take a couple of officers along. I will wait at the telephone till you get back."

Krag waited in great agitation. His face wore an expression of painful surprise and excitement. The Chief of Police stepped over to him and looked at him questioningly.

"Something must have gone wrong," said Krag.

"What could have happened?" asked the Chief.

But Krag only shook his head.

The whole company now waited in silence for the solution of the riddle. Even the millionaire, who did not understand the language which Krag and his Chief were speaking, felt that this strange affair which concerned him as well as the others had taken a new turn, and that something quite unexpected and out of the ordinary had occurred.

At last the telephone buzzed. The voice which had been speaking was audible once more.

"Well?" Krag questioned, impatiently.

"It is all very strange," replied the voice. "There were supposed to be four persons in the auto, were there not?"

"Certainly."

"Well there are only three in it. And they . . ."

"What do the three look like?" Krag interrupted.

"First of all there are our two policemen. And sitting beside them is an unknown man who is your very image. He is handcuffed."

"Where is the fourth?"

"I don't know."

"But what do the policemen in the auto say?"

"They don't say a word."

"Why not?"

"Because all three men are asleep," answered the voice.

Krag confined himself to asking: "Have they been taken into the building?"

"Yes, this very minute."

"And they are still sleeping?"

"Yes, it seems impossible to awaken them. They seem to be in a sound, normal sleep. Their breathing is regular, and there is nothing out-of-the-way about their appearance. But it is impossible to wake them up."

"Then I will come to headquarters at once," said Krag. "Hold the chauffeur and let the auto wait."

"Yes, sir. But what are we to do with the three?"
"Let them sleep," answered the detective.

The Chief of Police was already at the door, impatiently waiting for the end of the telephone conversation.

Krag bade the American a brief farewell, and promised to explain the whole matter to him later; and the American pushed him out of the door with friendly zeal, and begged him to make haste.

During the entire trip Krag said not a word, but looked attentively at all the people passing along the street on foot or in other cars.

When his car stopped in front of headquarters, he noticed that a policemen was guarding the yellow taxi.

When he entered the office on the ground floor he saw the three sleeping men, each of them stretched out on a couch. Their faces were quiet and composed, their cheeks were flushed with healthy color, like children sleeping the sleep of innocents.

But otherwise great excitement prevailed in the rooms. No one knew what kind of a crime had been committed, and the three silent, sleeping men who had arrived in the auto lent the whole situation a touch of grotesque mystery.

Asbjörn Krag said nothing further, but his face grew very serious once he had examined the three sleepers. The Italian seemed to be sleeping even

more soundly than the others. Several times Krag
shook them with utmost violence, but made absolutely no impression on them. They kept right on
sleeping the sleep of the just.

Then Krag sent for a well-known physician,
known as a specialist in narcotics and poisons. It
was quite evident that this was a poisoning case of
a peculiar nature. It betrayed itself in a manner
which Krag had never yet encountered in all his
years of experience, and since there was no odor
about the sleepers' breath, he found it impossible to
arrive at a conclusion as to what had produced their
coma. He at once realized, however, that the
Italian as well as the two police officers, had been
the victims of the old gentleman's cunning.

While waiting for the physician to arrive, Asbjörn
Krag questioned the chauffeur. The detectives recognized him at once. He was an older man who
had frequently driven him, and who had once been
a cab-driver. Any connection between this decent
old hackman and the fantastic robber band seemed
out of the question. The chauffeur himself was so
completely astonished that it was hard to get anything out of him.

No, he had noticed nothing out of the way during
the whole time he had been driving.

"But why did you drive so slowly? Or did you
stop under way?" Krag asked.

The answer was as follows: He had driven slowly, said the chauffeur, because he had noticed that a sick old man was sitting in the auto, and did not want to add to his suffering by making quicker time than was necessary. No, he had not stopped anywhere on the way.

Had he heard any cries, shouts or noise of any kind?

No, nothing at all. Everything had been perfectly quiet. And he had been very much surprised when no one got out of the auto after he had stopped in front of police headquarters.

One of the patrolmen who had helped carry the sleepers out of the car said that the two police officers were sitting on the rear seat, each of them leaning comfortably in his own corner. It looked as though they had purposely made themselves comfortable in order to take a nap, and there was nothing at all about them to show that they had been caught off their guard. The handcuffed man was stretched out along the length of the front seat. It seemed as though he had lain down in order to enjoy his snooze to the best advantage.

While these facts developed, the physician arrived.

He carefully examined the sleepers, but could not at once come to a conclusion regarding them. Although he seemed to have formed a theory he begged to be allowed to examine the auto before committing himself. The auto was driven into the enclosed court of the headquarters building, and there the physician examined it in the presence of Asbjörn Krag.

The physician's sensitive nose soon caught a whiff of a definite odor. "Camphor," he murmured, and turned inquiringly to Krag.

Krag also noticed a faint suggestion of the drug.

"But you must confess, doctor," he said, "that camphor in itself would not produce such a result."

"Certainly not, but camphor has a powerful smell. It may have been used to hide another odor, a fainter one."

And Asbjörn Krag was obliged to admit the logic of this conclusion as he returned with the physician to the police-office.

There the latter busied himself with his patients. He gave them a hypodermic which had the effect of making them move and mutter a few inaudible words. Finally, after he had put various other resuscitating measures into effect, one of the police officers opened his eyes, but only to close them again immediately.

Yet the one moment had been enough for the doctor.

"Did you see his eyes?" he asked.

"Yes," Krag answered, surprised. "They seemed to have a yellowish tinge."

"Quite right. And that explains the whole matter. These men have been rendered unconscious by means of a very rare narcotic poison found only in India and Tibet. A few days ago, strangely enough, I read a description of it in an English medical journal."

"Is it dangerous?"

"Not at all when used in an isolated way. But the coma may last for several hours, if the only means to waken those who are unconscious is not employed."

"And what is that means?" Krag asked.

"Caffeine, nothing more nor less than caffeine! It is something that we doctors always carry along with us fortunately."

The doctor opened his leather medicine-case and began to fuss with his bottles and hypodermics.

While he was busy with them there was a knock at the door, and a policemen entered.

He had a report to make. The officer in question was a new man on the force and the circumstance that he took the liberty of interrupting so important a conference showed that his message must be important.

"I was told that there was a mix-up in connection with the yellow taxi," he said.

"Yes, a closed yellow taxi," was Krag's reply.
"Do you know anything about it?"

"Yes, I do."

"Well, tell us your story."

"I was standing on the corner of Theatre Street,
when I saw an auto drive slowly up Willow Avenue.
Since there was nothing to distract my attention at
the moment, I kept my eyes on the auto, and while
it turned off at the Governent Building, the door on
the left opened, and an old gentleman with a gray
beard stepped out on the dashboard, and on into the
street. The auto went on."

"Did you know the gentleman?"

"At first, when I saw him, I thought it must be
the Chief of Police, but when he stepped down into
the street I could see by his walk that I had been
mistaken."

"Then you saw him step down from the dashboard into the street?"

"Yes, after he had closed the auto door"

"And this did not attract the attention of the
passers-by?"

"It did, but since the man smiled and waved to
someone in the car, people thought it must be a joke
of some kind, and did not think any more about it.
Only the man's strange resemblance to the Chief of
Police roused my suspicions."

"Did you follow him?"

"Yes, I followed him. When he came to No. 70
Theatre Street, one of the old houses in the block,
he went in."

"And did you wait outside for him?"

"I waited outside. I thought it might be worth
while knowing whether he lived there, or whether he
was merely paying a call."

"How long did you wait?"

"About half an hour."

"Did he come out again?"

"No, he stayed in."

Krag reflected a moment. Then he asked:

"And did no people at all come out of the house?"

"Yes, four in all while I was waiting. There was
an old woman, a young girl with a basket on her
arm, some electrical worker or telephone repair man,
and finally a young man who looked like a clerk or
bookkeeper."

"Thanks," said Krag, and it was clear that he felt
encouraged. "You are a good observer, and yet you
have let them pull the wool over your eyes. I would
like to wager that the old man who went into the
house was one of the four persons who came out of
it. Perhaps it was the repair man, perhaps it was
the old woman. Who knows? But I am glad to
know what you have told me."

While Asbjörn Krag was busy listening to the
patrolman's report, the physician had been experi-

menting with the sleepers. On the advice of the Chief of Police he decided to first recall one of the two police officers to consciousness.

In the course of a few minutes, during which the man in question groaned loudly, he at last opened his eyes.

He looked around him confusedly. Finally he seemed to pull himself together. He sat up, stretched out his hands—and then at once sank back again.

Again the physician applied his restoratives, and in a few minutes more the officer had so far recovered that he was able to say:

"I see through him . . ."

And Krag understood what he meant.

CHAPTER VI

ASBJORN KRAG, although he disliked to admit it, was compelled to acknowledge that the more daring of the two swindlers had made a fool of him in an extremely clever fashion. Yet the whole affair had not been altogether disadvantageous for the detective: at any rate the police had captured the gang's second in command, the small, lively Italian Ferro, and one of his assistants, the red-haired waiter.

The Chief of Police asked Krag whether he wished to question the two prisoners more in detail, and Krag replied that there was one or two things he would like to ask them.

As soon as the Italian had washed off his make-up, he was led in to be examined.

He was a man of medium height, some thirty years of age, with black, restless eyes, and a nervous manner. He displayed the most finished courtesy toward the Chief and the other police officials. A curiously superior, almost triumphant smile was reflected in his features when he looked at Asbjörn Krag."

The detective thought to himself: Why is he so

158

pleased? Here he is, trapped, and he knows that the leader of his gang may be led in at any moment . . . His smile was very noticeable . . . Krag had a disagreeable presentiment that new surprises might be in store for him. In fact, this whole affair was unlike any other with which he ever had been concerned. It seemed to be a struggle with jugglers or acrobats rather than with criminals.

The suspect gave his name as Giovanni Ferro, born in Milan, in 1894. By profession he was an "artist smith."

Krag at once seized upon the word. An "artist smith?" said he. That is a very comprehensive term. Which particular branch of your art do you cultivate?"

"I am especially interested in jewelry," replied the Italian, "gates of ornamental iron-work, decorative work, ornamental doors . . ."

"And door-locks?" queried Krag.

The Italian raised his eyebrows. "It stands to reason that no branch of my craft is altogether unfamiliar to me."

And when did you give up the practise of your craft?"

"I never have entirely given it up."

"Yet lately you have been practising another more remunerative trade?"

"That is not the correct name for it," answered

the Italian, suddenly turning serious, as though he were concerned, first of all, to see that all his answers were absolutely exact.

"What would you yourself prefer to call it then?" Krag asked.

"I should prefer to say that I had found a more interesting occupation."

"That is to say you became a criminal."

The Italian shrugged his shoulders. "It is very evident," he remarked, "that I am in the Far North."

"How so?"

"Your expressions no longer have the flexibility of those used in the Latin countries. I am a criminal and yet no criminal."

"That sounds very mysterious. Won't you explain yourself a little more in detail?"

The Italian seemed to reflect for a few moments. Finally he appeared to have arranged his thoughts to his liking. "I will take the theft in the home of the Chief of Police as an example," he said.

"Then you admit the theft in question?" Krag asked.

"Yes," answered the Italian, "I admit the theft solely in order to be able, using it is an example, to make perfectly clear to you what I mean."

"You are extremely generous."

"That is quite possible. You will confess that this theft, in particular, was a very daring one. It was nothing more nor less than putting one's head into the lion's mouth. It was the most difficult and dangerous thing we could have attempted. In fact, it would have been easier for us to have cleaned out the Bank of Norway than to have robbed the Chief of Police of all his furniture. And furthermore, you will have to admit that the advantages to be gained were quite out of proportion to the danger involved. To be frank, it was a decidedly unprofitable theft, for we could not dispose of the furniture or get it out of town. You must take that into consideration. Yet without any prospect of actual gain, we carried out one of the most desperate and dangerous burglaries which a human brain could conceive. We robbed the Chief of Police himself. In a manner of speaking this was a crime, yet you will have to admit that it was a crime with modifications. And another, more southern, more temperamental point of view would have found a more subtle and exact word of expression to describe it."

Krag smiled: "Then you mean to imply that this burglary was a kind of burglary for amusement's sake. The whole thing was staged for the sake of excitement and stimulation, or for variety's sake?"

The Italian seemed to give this serious consideration.

"It is difficult to define off-hand the reasons which motived it," he said. "All that I can tell you is that criminal motives, in the ordinary sense of the phrase, did not enter into the case. Perhaps a poet gifted with great intuition, some distinguished psychologist and artist, might present our motives in an understandable way."

The Chief of Police, who had been listening to this conversation, shook his head. "The man is playing a part," he said. "He wants to be sent to an asylum for observation in order to be able to escape the more easily. That is quite evident."

But the Italian quickly answered:

"I caught a single phrase, gentlemen: 'playing a part.' I can assure you that this is out of the question. I am not playing a part. Your supposition is an insult. I am just as sane as you are, gentlemen. I might even say that in some respects I am more intelligent. If I am to be subjected to these insults in the future I shall have to consider very seriously whether or no I will have anything further to say at all."

The Italian's haughtiness as he said this was quite indescribable. Asbjörn Krag studied him attentively.

"I perfectly agree with what you say regarding the burglary in the home of the Chief of Police," Krag then remarked. "This burglary could not have netted you very much, and its description makes it seem altogether devoid of sense. But the other thefts, the pockets picked at the poker-evening, for instance . . ."

"That is something I know nothing about."

"But we have all the proof we need in the shape of the letters sent by yourself and your leader."

"I have nothing to say."

"Have you ever been punished before?"

"Punished? I? Impossible!"

"The Italian shook his head, apparently deeply hurt.

"Do you mean to tell me," Krag asked with a smile, "that this is your first offence? Do you mean to say that this is the first time that you, the cleverest, most cunning thief I ever have met, have come in contact with the law?"

"No, it is not the first time. That stands to reason."

"What other crimes have you on your conscience?"

" 'Crimes?' My dear sir, I must object to that word. It once more makes me wish that some poetically gifted psychologist were my lawyer."

Krag turned to the Chief of Police: "Do you know," he said, "I have a feeling he has some definite object in view in all this talk. Perhaps he is merely trying to gain time."

The detective looked at his watch: "It is half-past four," he said.

And this gave rise to a very curious scene.

The Italian also drew a watch from his pocket. It was a watch with a nickel chain, of a make sometimes facetiously called a "turnip."

"Half-past four," he repeated and nodded his head.

The Chief of Police and the other officials looked at him with surprise. When he had been searched, everything of value had been taken from him, even a pocket-mirror. And here he suddenly pulled a watch out of his pocket.

It was then that the silence was interrupted by one of the police officers. "Why," he cried, "the fellow has *my* watch!" And quite out of countenance, the man felt in his empty pockets.

Then the rascal turned to him and handing him the watch said with a captivating, humorous smile: "Yes, it is your watch. Excuse me, but it is not good enough for me!"

Hesitatingly the officer accepted the time-piece. It was while he was being searched and while everything was being taken from him that the thief had nabbed the watch.

Asbjörn Krag could not help smiling.

"Would you call that a theft, too?" asked the Italian.

"I should call that a masterpiece of pickpocketing," said the detective, "and I am very glad to think we have at last secured you. I think the international police will congratulate us."

"You are quite mistaken," replied Ferro, with an injured air. "You are mistaken on all three counts, my dear sir. In the first place, I was not picking a pocket, but merely trying out an experiment; secondly, it was no masterpiece, but a very ordinary trick which the Russians carry out far more skilfully than we other Europeans, and thirdly, you have no reason whatever to congratulate yourself on having caught me. For you will not keep me very long."

"Do you expect to be able to prove your innocence?" asked Krag.

"Not at all," replied the Italian, "but I expect to escape soon."

"Indeed. That is quite an ambitious plan."

The Italian looked earnestly at Krag. "In the writing desk of your study is the cross of a decoration. It is set with brilliants. Am I right?"

Krag nodded.

"Very well. Inside of three days I will steal that decoration, after I have escaped from jail through my own efforts. Would you also call that a crime?"

"No, I should call that insanity."

"Then permit me to express myself more clearly. And I will not use so vague an expression as 'three days.' I will rob you of your decoration on the night of September fourth."

A silence fell on the whole room at this remarkably impudent declaration.

The officials looked at one another and smiled. Never in their lives had they encountered so phenomenal an impudence. Was the fellow joking? He had expressed himself in the most positive manner. Nor did he seem to speak in jest, though a certain amusement shone in his dark, animated face. And during the entire time his eyes never left those of Asbjörn Krag. It was evident that the daring rascal regarded Asbjörn Krag as his real antagonist.

The latter sat for a time in silence. He was pondering. At last he rose and said: "This examination is leading to no result. The man is only making fools of us. Take him off to the finger-print division. But be careful. It would be quite like him to try to carry out his threat. Has he been assigned a cell?"

"Yes," was the answer. "His cell is waiting for him."

"Which cell have you given him?"

"No. 34, in the upper corridor." It will be impossible for him to get out."

"Very well. Take him away. As soon as we have his finger-prints and his photograph we will at once notify the big capitals, Paris first of all. I think it will not be long before we get news of some of his Boulevard accomplishments."

Three police officers took hold of the prisoner.
He jerked away from them as though he objected
to having hand laid on him.

"Is this necessary?" he asked, turning to Krag.
"I give you my word that I will make no attempt
to escape."

Krag nodded. "Yes," he answered, "is is necessary."

"Then I will go," replied the man and took a
step forward. But he seemed to have been standing so long that his legs were asleep. For he stumbled and fell against Asbjörn Krag, who caught him
in his arms.

For a moment all in the room were surprised;
while the pickpocket overwhelmed the detective with
excuses.

"I hope I did not startle you," he said to Asbjörn
Krag. "It was very clumsy of me. But I am a
bit faint."

But as he spoke the same strange smile once more
flitted across his face.

Some presentiment made Krag feel for his watch.
Did the man really want to repeat the same old
trick?

But no, his watch was in its place.

The pickpocket noticed Krag's movement and
understood it. He bowed. "You are mistaken,"
he said. "I am no professional thief. And since

I shall be sitting in a cell for a while the passing of time for the moment does not interest me. I suppose there is a little sun in the room now and then?

Krag nodded.

"Then I can tell about what time it is from the position of the sunlight. I do not need to know exactly. But I shall steal your watch in the course of a few days. Or some one else's watch. For I cannot do without a watch indefinitely."

He made a ceremonial farewell bow and disappeared, surrounded by the three policemen. Krag could hear the echo of his footsteps die away on the stone floor.

When he was alone with the Chief of Police he said: "That was a very curious performance. I saw clearly that he did not really stumble, for I was watching him keenly the whole time. He was playing a part. But to what end? What was his purpose?"

"See whether you have your bill-fold," said the Chief with a smile. "I would not put anything past so clever a fellow."

Krag looked, but his bill-fold and all his papers were in his pocket. Nothing had been stolen from him. Was the whole thing a bit of foolery, carried out merely to confuse the police? And who or what was behind it all?

Now Krag and the Chief counted up the results of the day's work.

They had discovered the gang's main rendezvous in State House Street. Probably they would find the Chief's stolen furniture there.

They had laid hands on two members of the gang, the genial pickpocket Ferro and the red-haired gangster who had been masquerading as a waiter in the Continental Hotel.

It was not a bad beginning. Yet the gang leader himself, whose intention it was to plunder all Christiania, had thus far escaped them. But they were on his trail. The patrolman who had reported the incident in the Theater Street had plainly indicated where future investigations should be made.

Asbjörn Krag wished to lose no time going to Theater Street in order to see what could be done there. Meanwhile the Chief with a few of his men would make a thorough examination of the suspicious house in State House Street.

When Krag left police headquarters and stepped out on the street, another strange thing happened.

He was about to turn into Young Street when he saw a crowd gathering on the corner.

At the moment there were not so many people on the street, and yet quite suddenly this crowd seemed to have gathered on the corner.

Krag bumped against one of the crowd, and had

to clutch his hat lest it fall from his head. The next moment the whole crowd had melted away, and the people near him—ordinary, everyday people who apparently were passing by chance—went their way with exclamations of annoyance, a curse or an apology.

Instinctively Krag again felt for his watch and his bill-fold. They were still in his pockets. And yet he felt a certain unease. What was it? What had happened? No, nothing could have happened. And yet it was in the air, he knew that something was not in order. He looked around. Was he being followed? No, there was nothing to indicate it. Christiania Street looked just as it always did. The sidewalk showed the usual thin trickle of persons coming and going in the oblique rays of the sinking sun. Krag went ahead quickly. It was six o'clock.

He did not know the house in Theater Street for which he was hunting . . . he never had been there. But he knew its type. It was one of those houses that dated back to the middle of the nineteenth century. They all were three-storied buildings with narrow, creaking stairs and small halls.

He rang the bell on the ground floor, and asked the lady who opened the door who was living in the apartment, pretending that he was an official of the census bureau. She replied that she occupied the house with her son, who was an actor. Krag knew the names, and noted them down on a slip of paper. No, she did not sublet any rooms.

"Who lives above you?" he asked.

"Dr. Saling," was the answer.

Krag also knew his name, for it was one eminent in scientific circles. Dr. Saling was an old, wealthy eccentric whose research work in Egyptian archaeology had given him a position of distinction among Egyptologists. He was totally unknown to the general public.

When Krag rang Dr. Saling's housekeeper came to the door.

As soon as this lady caught sight of Krag she started and tried to shut the door in his face, but Krag quickly put his foot in it. He at once recalled her face. It was familiar to him, but he did not remember where he had seen it.

Is Dr. Saling in?" he asked.

"No," answered the lady, who by now had regained her self-control. She smiled in a kindly manner and added: "You must excuse me, but I was frightened when I saw you."

And now Krag knew who she was. She was a friend of his own landlady, and he had seen her in his own house off and on.

"Has anything happened?" she asked, somewhat disturbed. "Has anything happened to the Doctor?

He is so absent-minded. And at the present moment he had so much on his mind."

"Please let me in," Krag answered, "and then I will be able to set your mind at rest without delay."

She at once asked him to enter, and Krag passed through various rooms filled with a most curious collection of antiquities. The detective felt as though he were strolling through an Egyptian museum. He was especially interested in two mummies which stood in a dusty glass case.

At length they reached the dining-room. This was the housekeeper's domain. There were no curiosities there. Only objects such as one might expect to find in any dining-room.

The housekeeper begged Krag to be seated and he did so.

"Why," he asked, "has the Doctor so much on his mind just now?"

"Because he has a visitor from abroad. A very learned Frenchman is in Christiania, who has come here expressly to confer with the Doctor."

A curious restlessness took possession of Krag. Was it possible that the indefinite something which had been in his mind, off and on, for the past few hours, was beginning to take shape?

After he has begged the housekeeper to sit down near him, he said: "I shall tell you—but, of course, you must not breathe a word of it to any one—

that I am trailing a criminal who has committed some forgeries. And all that I know about him is that he had been living or staying for several days in a house here in Theater Street."

"It could not possibly be this house," said the housekeeper and shook her head with its white cap.

"That is something you cannot be too sure of," replied Krag. "The widow Salmon and her son, the actor, live below you, do they not?"

"Yes, but they have no boarders. So they could not be the ones."

"And it could not be the Egyptologist, either?"

The housekeeper turned pale. "That honest old man," she said. "I do not think you should talk in any such thoughtless way!"

"And the third story?"

"The owner of the house himself, together with his wife, his two sons and a young lady from Christiansund, a relative, live there."

"That is not at all satisfactory," murmured Krag. "Now I have made a house to house investigation of the street without the least result. Have the people on the third floor any lodgers?"

"No, the young lady is the only person living with them. She is only staying in Christiania to attend a school of art embroidery."

Krag rose with a sigh of resignation, and murmured:

"Then I shall have to give up this house, and try the next. It is a tiresome piece of work. But remember: Don't say a word to the Doctor about my being here!"

"No, no! Besides, it would not interest him at all."

Then Krag suddenly changed his tone and dropped business:

"When are you coming to see my landlady again?" he asked. "You have not paid us a visit for a long time."

"I should like to very much," said the housekeeper. "Your landlady is one of my best friends. But just at the moment I find it so hard to get – away."

"How is that?"

"Dr. Salinger has his company."

"Oh, I see."

"Yes, the French gentleman."

"What is his name?"

"Mr. d'Albert."

"Really?" cried Krag. "Why he is the famous Paris Egyptologist! That is very interesting. Is he living here with the Doctor?"

"No. He is staying at the Victoria Hotel, but he visits us every day. He is taking dinner with the Doctor tonight at seven o'clock."

"Then you have not much time left," said Krag.

"Otherwise I would have enjoyed taking a look at the Doctors' collections. I happen to be very much interested in Egyptian antiquities."

"But the Doctor never allows strangers to examine his collection. Even Mr. d'Albert would not have seen them had he not explained that he had come purposely from Paris to confer with the Doctor."

"Was he here today?"

"No, not today, so far as I know."

"What do you mean by 'so far as I know'?"

"Well, you see, the Doctor has his interests, and Mr. d'Albert has his own affairs to which to attend. And they do not interfere with one another. They are both very learned men, who often sit lost in thought for hours. In order that they will not disturb each other the Doctor has given Mr. d'Albert a key to the house. It often happens that I find him sitting in his room when I come in with letters, and that he has disappeared again without my knowing anything about it."

"Then, perhaps, he is sitting there now?"

"No, I am quite sure he is not, for I was in the room a moment ago and he was not there."

"Then perhaps you will let me drop in some other day and look at the collection?"

"If only I dared . . ."

"Why, it is perfectly safe! You know who I am.

So you may look to see me happen in some day when
the Doctor is not at home.   Suppose we say some
afternoon, about four."

"Yes, he never is at home then.   That is, if I can
risk . . ."

Asbjörn Krag said no more about it.   He acted
as though it were settled that he could come, and
took leave of the amiable housekeeper.

He made no further examination of the building,
but when he reached the street caught a passing taxi
and drove direct to the telegraph office.   There,
after a moment's thought, he sent the following telegram to an acquaintance of his on the Paris police
force: "Please investigate whether there is in Paris
an Egyptologist by the name of d'Albert.   If not,
please let me know whether any other French Egyptologist has gone to Christiania recently in order to
examine a private collection of Egyptian antiquities."

Then he went to the Victoria Hotel.   He soon
found out that a French scholar by the name of
Professor Armand d'Albert had been staying there
for some time.

He was a man of approximately fifty, he was told,
with a greyish beard, powerful glasses and in every
way the typical research worker and scholar in appearance—absent-minded, exact, extremely correct.
He came in at certain definite hours, and his life
seemed regulated by clock-work.   He had valuable

Egyptian art objects in his room, and had given the most positive orders that no stranger was to enter it.

"But if the police wish . . ." said the house detective, "of course . . ."

"This is positively no police inquiry," said Krag. "I have a purely personal interest in inquiring. I am anxious to confer with him regarding a scientific matter.

"Very well," said the house detective with a wink. "I understand perfectly. The police are not interested in Mr. d'Albert."

Meanwhile it already was half-past seven, and Asbjörn Krag drove home. On his desk he found a report from the Chief of Police. The house in State Street had been searched and the more valuable articles of furniture stolen from the Chief's home had been found. But otherwise the nest was empty, and the birds had flown. Not one of the gang had been seen. The Chief had posted men, however, to watch for them.

Not a single scrap of paper, not a letter or document of any kind had been discovered which might throw some light on this mysterious band which had so suddenly transferred its activities to Christiania.

Krag laid the report aside. It was surprising how suddenly he seemed to have lost the swiftness and energy which usually marked his working methods.

A man who knew him well would have thought that he had completely run himself aground, because he realized that he was dealing with a new type and kind of criminal.

But the truth was that the whole matter had taken a new turn altogether that afternoon, and had assumed an entirely different character.

Krag was more than ever interested, but at the same time he found himself further than ever removed from any logical solution.

Quite suddenly he was no longer nearly as eager to catch the captain of the gang, the famous "Mr. Raspail," the sick Frenchman who had so cleverly escaped from the auto.

While he sat smoking his pipe after dinner his housekeeper entered the room with a telegram.

It was a local telegram, and its contents greatly surprised the detective. For it read: "My best thanks for the communication you were kind enough to pass on to me from the prisoner in cell No. 34. Take good care of the decoration in the lower left-hand drawer of your writing-desk. The Man for Whom You Are Looking."

Krag read the telegram several times in succession. And the more carefully he studied it the more surprised he became. The prisoner in cell No. 34 was Ferro.

But had he—Krag—carried a message from the

jailed pickpocket? And to whom? Who was the man for whom he was looking?

The telegram must have been sent by the leader of the gang, thought Krag. And then he mentally reviewed all that had taken place that afternoon.

He dwelt on two points in particular. The prisoner's strange manner when he had stumbled. And —the crowd on the corner of Moller and Young Streets when he had passed that way.

Asbjörn Krag rose.

Yes, there was no getting away from it. He himself, the detective, had quite unwittingly carried an important message to the chieftain of the gang.

CHAPTER VII

THE JEWEL ROBBERY

DURING the next few days Krag continued his secret investigations with great zeal. At police headquarters surprise was expressed at his taking so little interest in the examination and depositions of the two arrested masqueraders. He hardly ever appeared to listen to the proceedings.

He wandered about quite on his own hook. From time to time he would pop up in the most unexpected localities in town. Police officials mentioned catching sight of him several times. Once they had seen him hanging around a brickyard. Again he had been glimpsed down on the water-front, watching the loading of a steamship bound for Antwerp.

He seemed to have no special object in view of these excursions of his. He merely watched and registered his observations silently, without saying a word to any one. It was also said at police headquarters that he had taken a room in the Victoria Hotel.

Incidentally, the two men arrested were a thorn in the flesh of the investigating judge. They had a thousand and one equivocations and excuses, and made the most fantastic statements in order to confuse the minds of their examiners, so that the judge was unable to see a single ray of light in the darkness they spread over the proceedings.

Both seemed to have made up their minds to play a part, with malice aforethought, in order to make the work of the court as difficult as possible.

The Italian in this police comedy assumed the rôle of the fussy society man about town.

At the beginning of every examination he registered a complaint against the unsatisfactory condition of his cell, the poor quality of the soap and the wretched toilet necessities supplied him. Shaking his head mournfully, he would look at his fingers, and regret bitterly that it was impossible for him to keep his nails properly manicured.

When finally he was induced to speak about his offences against the law, he immediately began to boast and lie to such an extent that the judge was entirely at a loss. Two days passed and each day, when he was questioned, he repeated that he expected to make his escape.

The red-haired waiter had an altogether different rôle. He looked and acted the part of the natural-born fool with the most convincing mimicry. When he was questioned with regard to his part in the strange and daring series of robberies, he first pretended that he did not know what he was being he was mistaken for anything but a waiter. And asked. Then he would seem to be surprised that this monument of pretended stupidity shed all questions like a duck's back does water, till the judge felt he could draw more even from the Italian's extravagant falsehoods, than from the red-haired man's affected innocence.

Under these circumstances the hour when Krag would at last break his silence, or the international police would give some signs of life, was looked forward to with longing. It was generally understood that Krag was following a clue in town which no one else knew about, and it as also known that the criminal police in Paris and London were investigating in an attempt to discover some particulars regarding the earlier life of the two men held.

Hence it is not hard to understand that the examining judge as well as the Chief of Police were impatient, and that they almost began to despair when they learned, privately, that Asbjörn Krag, for the moment, had devoted himself exclusively to Egyptological studies. He was spending hours in conference with the scholars at the University discussing the Egyptian treasures kept there. So one of the professors informed the Chief of Police when he met him one day in the street, not without surprise at the detective's sudden interest in the subject.

The next time the Chief of Police saw Krag he questioned him concerning it: "Why, I am studying

Egyptian antiquities merely to pass time," said Krag.

"To pass the time?" cried the Chief, astonished. "I must say I cannot see that just now you have any particular reason to feel bored."

"I am not bored," answered Krag.

"But how about taking a little more interest in the case of our two interesting friends in jail?"

"I think of no one else," was the detective's answer.

The Chief of Police looked at him, dumbfounded. Something about Krag's eyes struck him. He had already, on one or two other occasions, noticed that they had the same expression. The detective's glance was at once deep, weary and searching. It showed that Krag was not sleeping.

And then the Chief began to suspect that Krag was seeking the truth in strange and devious ways. He determined to rely upon him absolutely and wait, but his expectancy was pitched to high tension.

Yet the whole matter was one of hours rather than days. A strange restlessness had taken possession of police headquarters, usually so quiet and humdrum. Every one was on the alert for the arrival of telegrams and reports. During the preceding weeks reports of some crime committed had come in nearly every evening. Now, with the arrest of the three suspects, a sudden and threatening

quiet had developed. And it had a very depressing
effect, since it was known that the leader of the
gang, the strange individual who planned their
crimes, was still at liberty. Where was he? What
were his plans? How could he escape Asbjörn
Krag, the man knew his Christiania, which was,
after all, not such a large city, as he did his own vest
pocket? These were the questions asked, and when
from hour to hour, instead of an answer, the same
ominous silence continued unbroken, astonishment
and tension rose to feverish heights. All felt that
they were powerless where this mysterious criminal
was concerned.

The authorities were convinced that the gang
which had been operating with such astonishing impudence had suffered a great setback. At the same
time, however, every one sensed that it had not been
completely broken up. And that is why the unbroken
silence weighed so heavily on all those interested.

For this reason it was an actual relief when, finally,
at noon of the second day after the arrests had been
made, the gang once more showed signs of life.

For the first time one of their attempts had been
foiled. And this circumstance led the Chief of Police to guess—though he did no more than guess—
that his men, after all, had captured the gang leader
in the person of the Italian Ferro.

A robbery had been committed in a jewelry store

in one of the most frequented business streets of
Christiania. But the thief had gone to work in so
clumsy a manner that he had at once been arrested.

He pretended that he was a representative of the
Countess Esterhazy who, according to his statement,
was staying at the Grand Hotel. He stepped into
the jewelers' with an authorization from her to examine some jewels she wanted to purchase.

Since he had a confident, prepossessing manner
and made a good impression he was not suspected
for a moment.

But while he was selecting a necklace from an
assortment shown him, one of the salesmen noticed
that he improved the opportunity to drop a diamond
ring into his pocket. The salesman quietly informed
the head of the firm, and the latter at once sent for
the police. An officer promptly appeared, and it
was at once clear to him that the case was one of an
ordinary, everyday attempt at robbery. The diamond ring was found in the man's pocket, and in
spite of his noisy and exaggerated protests he was
taken to the police station.

In itself such a case was not especially interesting, since there was no object in denying the attempted crime. Nor did the thief make any attempt to do so. As mute as an oyster he confronted
the officer who examined him, and acted as though
he did not know what it was all about. He declared

that his name was Vinner and that he came from Alsace, and he would not say another word.

On the other hand, a curious manoeuvre of his attracted attention. He made an attempt to drop a small package behind the stove in the room in which he was examined. One of the patrolmen present at once retrived the package.

It contained about twenty ordinary visiting-cards. On each of them was printed: "The Man Who Plundered the City."

The cards had been printed in a hand-press, and the individual letters were not straight. It was clear that the printing had been done by an inexperienced hand.

After this discovery the examination took on a livelier turn, and the greatest pressure was exerted to compel the arrested man to make some disclosure of value; but he persisted in his obstinate silence.

Krag was telephoned for and messengers sent in search of him, but he was nowhere to be found.

At last nothing remained but to lock the fellow up in a cell as far as possible removed from that in which Ferro was kept.

At eight o'clock that evening Asbjörn Krag was at last discovered. He had just returned from some mysterious expedition. He was at once informed of what had taken place, but, strange to say, it did not seem to interest him in the least.

When the Chief of Police asked him what was next to be done, he merely replied that for the present no steps of any kind need be taken.

He was waiting for something to happen, and the happening or which he was waiting duly took place.

* * *

In addition to the mysterious visiting-cards which had been found in the possession of the arrested Alsatian, there also had been some letters, addressed to Mr. Charles Thollon, General Delivery, Christiania.

The police at once sent for the head of the general delivery department in the Christiania Post Office, and the latter recognized the prisoner himself as the man who called for the letters addressed to Mr. Thollon. The deceiver's clumsiness was once more laid bare. Not only had he gone about carrying out his trumpery robbery in the most stupid way, but he also had been foolish enough to carry the compromising cards about with him in his pocket. Still more foolish, however, had been his giving a fictitious name when he knew he would be searched, and the self-addressed letters, letters which showed that at some previous time, at all events, he had gone under the name of Charles Thollon, would be found on his person.

This appeared to the police to be a very strong chain of circumstantial evidence, and when Asbjörn

Krag appeared and learned the result of the examination, he smiled.

Krag stepped up to Thollon and looked him over carefully. The criminal did not wink an eye. He merely stared vacantly before him. His face, for the moment, showed such an expression of concentrated stupidity that Krag was almost inclined to believe he was absolutely and hopelessly a nit-wit.

In order to be on the safe side, one of the men had telephoned to the Grand Hotel to obtain information from the Countess Esterhazy, since the thief had pretended to be acting in her name. Of course, the answer had been that the lady did not know him, and had not contemplated making any purchase of jewelry.

After a consultation with Krag the Chief of Police decided to confront Thollon with the Italian who was under arrest. Even though it was doubtful whether anything were to be gained by this move, it seemed worth trying. Two policemen were sent to bring in the lively and daring Italian. In the meantime Thollon was led to one side, so that Ferro would not see him as he entered the room. The police had decided that an unexpected meeting would give them the best results.

Mr. Thollon had no idea at all what was in the wind, as was easily to be seen by the mask of stupidity he had assumed. He made not the least attempt to disobey the orders of the officials and, though surprised, did as they told him quite willingly. He was placed between the wall and a wardrobe in such a way that the latter hid him. Then he was told to keep his mouth shut until he was questioned.

No sooner had these preparations been made than the door opened and the lively little Italian, escorted by two policemen, entered. He greeted those present politely, though somewhat formally, and when he caught sight of Asbjörn Krag a fleeting smile crossed his face.

"We would like to know," said the investigating judge, "whether you have any further revelations to make at the present time?"

The Italian raised his eyebrows. "Why at the present time?" he inquired.

"Something has happened which makes it seem advisable for you to confess the whole truth."

The Italian smiled. "No doubt you have received information concerning me from abroad, from Paris or Rome for example?"

"What do you say that? Do you imagine that any information of the kind would be of advantage to you?"

"That depends altogether upon one's point of view," was his reply.

"One's point of view?"

"Exactly! From which side of the fence one is looking at the matter. I take for granted that you already have received information regarding me from Paris. The Paris police work quickly. Supposing they have sent you word that I am a daring, dangerous thief, an impudent and cunning criminal, one able to deceive even the cleverest persons. In that event I would say that the information was to my advantage. I should feel flattered by being so highly complimented. You, sitting on the other side of the fence, however, would say that my character testimony was a disadvantage to me. For, as I have said, it is practically impossible to express one's self positively in a case where people look at circumstances in so different a way."

When the Italian had finished his little speech he looked around with a proud smile, as though expecting to be applauded. And the police were not a little surprised, for this was a philosophy which criminals did not as a rule express at a hearing.

But instead of answering him the judge made a motion, and suddenly the Italian found himself face to face with Thollon.

The effect of the encounter exceeded the fondest hopes of the police.

The faces of both criminals displayed the most unbounded astonishment.

The next moment, however, their expressions

changed. The Italian's eyes sparkled with annoyance and rage. Thollon's eyes, on the other hand, were not visible at all, for he hung his head with the deepest humility and discouragement. And he was heard to murmur, in French: "Forgive me!"

For a short time the Italian looked at him with contempt, then he shrugged his shoulders and turned to the judge: "Is that your surprise?" he asked, sarcastically.

"It seems to have made an impression on you," replied the magistrate.

"No doubt, for if you meant to surprise me I might as well admit that you have been entirely successful."

"Do you know the man?"

"Yes."

"What is his name?"

"Thollon, Charles Thollon."

"Is he one of your colleagues?"

An expression of supreme contempt glided over the Italian's face. "No," he replied and he emphasized the word as though to say that nothing could be more improbable.

"Who is he, in that case?"

"Have you not yet found out?"

"No."

"He is the greatest simpleton in Europe."

"That is no explanation. You admit knowing

him.   He must be connected in someway or other
with your comrades and yourself."

"Yes, he is connected with us exactly as a servant
is connected with his master."

"Well, well, then your gang even keeps its own
servants?"

"He is our leader's servant."

Thollon started, then cast a reproachful glance
at his fellow-prisoner.

The judge turned to Thollon.   "Is he telling the
truth?" he asked.

A deep groan burst from Thollon's lips.   "Yes,
he is," he replied.

"What is your master's name?"

The Italian was about to speak, but the judge
prevented this.

"What is your master's name?" he repeated.

The servant lowered his head and whispered a
name, yet so indistinctly that the judge was obliged
to repeat his question another time.

He hesitated for a moment.

"His name is Raspail," he finally said.

This was a disappointment to those present, for
they had expected to hear some other name mentioned.

"Did he send you out to steal?"

The servant sadly shook his head.   He was evidently growing more nervous and restless, and his

fingers began to beat a tatoo on the smooth surface of the closet wardrobe.

"Then how did you come to commit your theft?"

"It was my own idea."

"Very well, but why?"

"Because I had no money."

"Has your master no money?"

"Yes, a great deal of it."

"Then you could have obtained some from him, could you not?"

"No," replied the servant, "I could not."

"Why not?"

"Because my master had left me."

"So that's it! And where does he live?"

"At the Hotel Malmo, on the harbor."

The judge made note of the name on a slip of paper, and handed it to an officer who at once disappeared with it.

"When did your master desert you?"

"Three days ago."

The Chief of Police nodded and his eyes sought those of Asbjörn Krag. To his great surprise he saw that the latter was staring at the prisoner's hands.

Suddenly the detective cried "Stop! These two rascals are talking to each other!"

For half a second a gleam of intelligence, a swift, watchful look, appeared in the simple servant's eyes.

But immediately after he shook his head as though he did not understand, and let his lower jaw hang like some idiot in a fit of deep brooding.

The judge straightened up in his seat and looked curiously at Thollon and Krag while he asked for an explanation.

Then Krag said, softly: "I suspect that they are turning our investigation into a farce. While you were questioning the man who goes under the name of Thollon, I have been watching his fingers."

"Yes, the man is evidently nervous."

"Take a good look at this tall, strong fellow, with his sane, quiet, stupid eyes. Do you really think that a man can be highly nervous with such a physique?"

"Perhaps not. What is the matter with his fingers?"

"For the last five minutes he has been moving them in a peculiar way which seemed to indicate that he was talking to the other man."

"I see—and did the other fellow answer him?"

"So far as I could make out he did not."

"In that case it does not seem probable that they have carried on a real conversation with each other.

"No, but it does seem as though the other had been given some information."

"Did you understand what the communications were?"

"Of course not."

"Why 'of course'?"

"In that case I should have let Thollon go right on talking. I think we have made a mistake in this matter."

"In what way?"

"In confronting the two with one another."

The judge looked dubious. "Then it also may have been a mistake to arrest this last man," he said somewhat sacastically. "I think we are looking at the case a bit too much as an international affair. I have some knowledge of human nature myself, and I must admit that I have seldom seen a more incredibly stupid and more inconceivably simple man than the one in front of us."

For a moment Krag did not reply, and then he asked: "Is it necessary to question this man any further before we get some news from the Hotel Malmo, where he lived with the leader of the gang?"

The judge looked from one to the other. "It seems to me," he answered, "that it would be easy for us to get this stupid fellow to make further additional admissions, but I can wait if the Chief of Police thinks it best.

The Chief of Police left it to Krag to decide.

"What do you think?" he asked.

"I should say wait," Krag replied.

The judge nodded. "Very well," he said, and ordered the prisoner led away.

Before this was done, however, Krag whispered to him: "Thollon must be put in one of the cells from five to nine, if one is empty. He must be placed as far as possible away from the others."

"Have it your own way," said the judge. "Those are matters in which I do not interfere."

Krag gave some orders and the prisoners were led away singly and jailed so far apart that it was impossible for them to communicate with each other.

As soon as the officials were alone the judge said: "And now I should like to have your opinion."

Krag replied: "I feel sure, just as I have already mentioned, that both these gentlemen were playing a farce exclusively for your benefit."

"I cannot agree with you," said the judge. "But here comes the man whom I sent to the Hotel Malmo. Let us hear what he has to say."

The policeman reported that two foreigners, as a matter of fact, had been recently staying at the hotel. One—his description agreed with that of Thollon—spoke only French. The other, evidently a man much higher in the social scale, also spoke some English and had used that tongue to make his wishes known to the hotel personnel.

"So far this all agrees with my own conclusions," remarked the judge. "Go on . . ."

"At the hotel the general impression was that the one man was the master and the other the servant. The master was often uncivil and abused his servant violently. And the latter always seemed very anxious to do exactly as his master wanted. I took special pains to ask the hotel staff what they thought of the servant, and they all agreed in describing him as not being very intelligent. At times he gave shocking exhibitions of stupidity, and would often stand about with his jaw hanging as though he had lost his wits."

The judge nodded in a satisfied way to Krag and said: "Continue!"

"Three days ago the master suddenly disappeared, and after that he never showed up again."

Here Krag inquired: "How did he disappear?"

"Well, they could not give me any satisfactory explanation as to that. One afternoon master and servant went out together, and neither one of them returned that night. It was around eleven o'clock in the forenoon of the following day that the servant returned home alone."

"Was there anything to show that something unusual had happened?"

"No, but in the course of the evening he began to ask after his master, and when the latter did not return the following day it was plain that the servant was much upset."

"And then?"

"Then the hotel people began to get suspicious and sent in their bill. This the servant at once paid, and gave liberal tips besides, which somewhat reassured them. Yet one curious incident happened."

"What was that?"

"That the gentleman's baggage also disappeared."

This circumstance rather upset the judge.

"Did he have much baggage?" asked Krag.

"No," said the police officer, who had made inquiries at the hotel, "only a small hand-bag. But that had disappeared. And with it all the owner's toilet articles, collars, ties and so forth."

"Did the master carry this hand-bag the evening he went out with his servant?"

"That no one at the hotel could say, for no one saw him leave. All they knew was that the two were in the hotel at four o'clock, and that at six, when some one went to their rooms, they were not there."

"Were they in the habit of going out together?"

"Very seldom."

"How did the servant act yesterday and the day before?"

"He grew more and more restless, and kept asking after his master. At least the hotel folks got the idea that he had no more money."

When he heard this the judge laid his hand down

on the court record. "There is the explanation, just as I thought. The master left the poor servant in the lurch. We may take for granted that this gentleman is identical with the old, invalid Mr. Raspail who was arrested in the Grand Hotel, together with the Italian. After he escaped from the hands of our police almost by a miracle, he did not wish to return to the hotel. Or else, he stole back secretly to get his bag, and then made a get-away. His stupid servant—so he calculated—would only have been a hindrance to him in his flight, and so he left him behind. Then the servant ran short, his money gave out, and when he had nothing left he attempted to carry out his idiotic robbery at the jeweler's. The mysterious visiting-cards, of course, were those of his master. We may take it for granted that he knew something of his master's affairs, and for that reason is not telling us anything at all, for fear he might betray too much. It seems clear as far as we have gone."

But Asbjörn Krag's dissatisfied face showed that this explanation did not satisfy him.

Suddenly the Chief of Police took a hand in the discussion. "There is another possible explanation. Is it not conceivable that these two men who confronted each other here a few moments ago were, respectively, the master and servant?"

Krag nodded his head eagerly. "I had thought

of that. It is an explanation which seems reasonable, but it has one weak point."

The judge was so surprised at the possibility which had been so suddenly indicated, that he sat in silent expectation, looking at his colleagues without uttering a word. There was something in the Chief of Police's tone which showed that he, too, did not consider the judge's theory acceptable. It appeared too simple.

"At first glance," said Krag, "it seems almost as though the two men who stood in front of us a short time ago were master and servant. In that case you would say, of course, that the Italian was the master, would you not?"

"Of course."

"That is open to question. However, admitting if for the sake of argument, the whole theory falls to the ground on a single count."

"And what is that?" asked the Chief of Police.

"You have completely forgotten the hand-bag," replied Krag. "They said at the Hotel Malmo that the hand-bag in the gentleman's room disappeared with its owner. But I do not think this happened the same day on which the gentleman was seen for the last time. I think it was taken from his room the day following."

"Then you think that the man whom we call the master went back secretly to the hotel the day after

the catastrophe in order to secure his hand-bag?"
asked the Chief of Police.

"No, I do not say that.   I think the servant
brought him the hand-bag."

"Then you think the servant had his master's new
address all the time?"

"If not all the time, he did know it a few days
after the Italian had been arrested."

"But in that case why did he grieve and ask after
his master?"

"Because he was playing a part."

"And why should he play a part?"

"Because he had been ordered to do so."

"Who had ordered him?"

"His master."

"But then can you tell me why he tried to carry
out that stupid robbery in the jeweler's shop?"

"The very fact that it was carried out so stupidly
explains everything.   He was again playing a part,
at his master's orders."

Here, however, the judge smiled and interrupted,
doubtfully: "But my dear sir, what you say is too
incredible.   Why should the master order his servant to commit this robbery?"

"Because the gentleman wanted his servant to
be arrested," said Asbjörn Krag.   "He was keen
to have the police gather him up.   You do not imagine for a moment that a gang of his sort carries

around a servant, do you? Besides, it is quite out
of reason to think that so imaginative and daring a
group of criminals includes a member so extraordinarily stupid as Thollon. He has a rare gift of
playing the part of a half-idiot and this gift, of
course, he uses for the benefit of himself and his
comrades. But I think that he is quite as clever as
the lively little Italian who seems to treat him with
such contempt."

"Up to this point your deductions may be logical," said the judge, who was beginning to get interested in Krag's exposition. "But it still seems to
me that the essential question must be: In the name
of common sense why should the leader wish to lose
another member of his band? Why did he want to
have Thollon arrested?"

Krag smiled: "That question is the easiest one of
all to answer."

The judge looked up at him.

"I have already mentioned," Krag continued,
"that I regard this servant who makes such a display of his stupidity, as bright as the little Italian.
I may exaggerate. Ferro is more intelligent, he is
a more useful member of the gang, and that is the
explanation in a nut-shell."

"Still I do not understand."

"It is beyond all doubt that they are planning to
break out of jail."

"Ah, I see."

"Ferro must be gotten out of jail, because his master needs him and because, from day to day, the reports of the international police concerning him may be expected to come in. The gist of the matter is that Thollon has allowed himself to be arrested at his master's command. His master knew that if the mysterious visiting-cards were found in his possession, it was very probable that we would confront him with Ferro. That would give Thollon an opportunity of giving Ferro whatever information the leader wished given him. You also may rest assured, gentlemen, that Ferro has received and understood this message. Criminals of this type have an alphabet of their own. It consists of a drumming with the fingers, a manner of winking with the eye-lids, a method of placing the feet together, a peculiar way of moving the arms, the angle the face forms with the chest. Those are all letters or sentences. We would be mistaken if we thought Thollon was restless or nervous. He was merely in the act of telegraphing some information to his friend and fellow-gangster. Unfortunately, I discovered what was going on too late, though during the whole time they were confronting each other I had a definite conviction that some rascality was going on before our very eyes. And that is the truth, gentlemen. If we look at matters in the right

way, everything dovetails: the master's disappear-
ance, the hand-bag, the uniquely clumsy attempt at
robbery, the mysterious visiting-cards, Thollon's in-
conceivable stupidity, they all fit together. We have
once more allowed ourselves to be fooled, and that
is the whole story."

The judge leaped violently to his feet: "Yes, you
are right!" he cried. "You must be right! Now
I can see the whole thing clearly. But I am not
the only one to have been fooled. All three of you
gentlemen are in the same position."

Krag let the judge's remark pass and once more
turned to the officer who had made the investigations at the Malmo Hotel. "Did you get a description of the hand-bag that disappeared from the
room?" he asked.

"Yes," answered the officer, as he glanced at his
notes, "though they could not give me an exact description, since it had not been closely examined.
It was a black leather bag, practically new, and with
a leather handle. A neat lithographed card was
fastened to the handle on which was the name
'Pierre Raspail,' and under it 'Lyon.' "

"Were any labels pasted on the bag?"

"There had been labels pasted on it, but they
had been scraped off, as the traces that were left
showed. Only one label had been left, and it was
easy to make it out. The hotel people said that it

was stamped 'Maltes Hotel, Nice.' I suppose that means the Hotel de Malte, Nice."

"Very likely."

"That was all the information I could secure. On the other hand, I brought along the servant's baggage!"

"Let us have a look at it!"

It consisted of a leather hand-bag, which might have resembled the one described by the officer, and attached to the handle was a visiting-card which read: 'Charles Thollon, Paris.' "

"A servant who uses the same style hand-bag and visiting-cards as his master," murmered Krag, "is a curiosity. And now we will see what it contains."

The hand-bag was opened and its contents dumped out upon the table, while all in the room crowded around with the greatest interest, the judge by no means the least eager. A hard object dropped on the table. Krag picked it up; it was a large, bluish-grey revolver of the heaviest calibre. Krag opened it. There were still five unused cartridges in the magazine.

"One shot has been fired," said Krag thoughtfully, as he laid the revolver aside. "I wonder whether it was discharged here in the city or not? Who can tell?

Then some underclothing appeared, of the finest quality, and quite new. The firm name was still on

the goods, and Krag read: "Magasin du Louvre."
"It seems as though we may take for granted," said
Krag, "that our robbers came direct from Paris.
And, furthermore, we also can take for granted that
this is no servant's outfit. Why, look at these goods,
they are the finest quality silk!"

Then Thollon's toilet-case was examined. It
looked far more as though it belonged to some young
man about town than to a thief. The case itself
was made of fragrant morocco leather, inlaid with
silver. The various combs and brushes it contained
were made of expensive woods with silver inlay.
And there were small bottles of toilet-water and per-
fumes of a very expensive make. It was all very
interesting, yet while it supported Krag's conten-
tions, it gave him nothing more definite to go on
with. In fact, after having examined the servant's
baggage, they were no further advanced than before.
Yet Krag appeared satisfied with the results of the
investigation so far.

"We have found two trails," he said, "one leads
backward, the other forward."

"How so?" asked the judge.

Krag pointed to the firm-label: "Magasin du
Louvre." Beneath it was printed "Rue de Havre".
This showed clearly that the goods had been pur-
chased in the great Paris department-store. "We
know that the thieves came from Paris, and that they

only left Paris a short time ago. That is the trail
which leads backwards."

"And the one that leads forward?"

"The hand-bag—the other hand-bag! It must
still be in the city, and I think I know where to look
for it!"

CHAPTER VIII

THE PARIS TRAIL

BEFORE we go on with our account of what happened in the police department building after the two mysterious criminals had been taken away to their cells, and what took place in Asbjörn Krag's home, we must take a closer look at Krag's activities in the Victoria Hotel.

We have already mentioned how the fact that Krag had settled down in this hotel had attracted attention at police headquarters. It was supposed that he was following some clue, and all were keyed up to hear of a discovery, for Krag had been living in the hotel for some time, and, as a rule, when he settled down anywhere, it was not long before something happened.

Now the detective had his suspicions regarding a gentleman in Room 24, a French scholar who appeared on the hotel register as Mr. d'Albert. During his first day at the hotel, Krag had found out that this man was the same professor who was at liberty to enter the house of the eccentric Dr. Saling in Theatre Street whenever he felt like it. Krag noted down the result of his investigations with much satisfaction.

First: When the gang leader had fled from the auto he had entered the house where the eccentric Dr. Saling lived.

Secondly: After repeated calls on Dr. Saling's house-keeper, Krag had discovered that a fair-sized trunk belonging to Mr. d'Albert was kept in the professor's rooms. According to what the house-keeper told him, this trunk contained rare scientific works which the two gentlemen used in their conferences regarding Egyptian dialects. Yet Asbjörn Krag had also come to the conclusion that the trunk might very easily contain articles of clothing, wigs, false beards, and the like. The lock resisted his best tools—and he did not want to break it.

Fourth: Mr. d'Albert had free access to the library, at all hours, and thence could pass into Dr. Saling's study room.

All this seemed to indicate that Mr. d'Albert might well be the leader of the gang.

When Krag had reached these conclusions he was startled, for he was at once compelled to confirm another series of facts equally undeniable:

First: The French police informed him that a philologist by the name of d'Albert actually did exist in Paris—a man who occupied no official position, and yet had a distinguished reputation in scientific circles. This d'Albert was a wealthy man and carried on his studies for the sake of science alone.

He already had spent a fortune in travel and investigation. When in Paris he lived in a very retired manner and saw practically no one. At the moment he was not in Paris (Was it because he was in Christiania?). The French police could not supply d'Albert's present address. Such was the information sent them from Paris.

Secondly: It could not be denied that the eccentric philologist in Theatre Street held long conferences with d'Albert on scientific subjects. This was indisputable evidence that d'Albert was really and truly the scientist he pretended to be.

Thirdly: D'Albert had on two different occasions visited the well-known professor of Egyptology at the University of Christiania, Professor C. T. A. Winger. This was the same Winger who had been a guest at Consul Birger's famous poker party, at which the impudent thief had stolen every one's money before the beginning of the game. Krag had hunted up Professor Winger, and the latter had told him that Mr. d'Albert, as a matter of fact, was very well· versed in Egyptian hieroglyphics, and even had been able to communicate some very valuable deductions to him.

All in all: While there were only a few vague indications to show that Mr. d'Albert might be the leader of the mysterious criminal gang, it was beyond dispute that he was the man he had given him-

self out to be, both at the hotel and to Dr. Salinger
—he was a scientist who had come to Christiania in
order to confer with colleagues studying his own
scientific subject.

Hence Krag acted only with the greatest circum-
spection. Several times he was almost tempted to
give up this particular trail altogether, yet a curious
subconscious instinct prevented him from so doing.
And then something happened which aroused Krag's
suspicions more than anything else had done. Mr.
d'Albert revealed himself in a very curious light.
He did so one Saturday evening, toward ten o'clock,
two days after the jewel-robber Thollon had been
arrested.

Krag had his *sub rosa* connections at the hotel. He
was not yet sure enough, with regard to his investigations, to be able to take the hotel management
frankly into his confidence. Hence he was supposed
to be living at the hotel for a time because of
strictly private reasons. This shows how careful he
was. He feared to attract attention at too early a
date. Instead, he had smuggled one of his assistants into the hotel as a waiter. It was his former
servant Jens, now the latest newcomer on the criminal detective staff. This young fellow, who was
devoted to Krag, reported to him almost hour by
hour what the Frenchman was doing. And since
Jens knew very well that his master attached impor-

tance to what seemed to the least important details, Krag found out when Mr. d'Albert deigned to eat breakfast, when he took his after-dinner nap, when he went out, how he was dressed, whether he took a taxi or went on foot, and so forth and so on.

Yet it is easy to understand that in spite of all this Krag was beginning to grow impatient. One hour followed another, the days went by, and still nothing happened. Therefore he was delighted when finally, on the Saturday in question, Jens at last informed him that a large-sized package had come for Mr. d'Albert from a little second-hand clothing shop in Grand Street.

Here we might remark that during the whole time of his stay at the hotel Mr. d'Albert had spoken nothing but French. Nor had he given a sign of understanding any other tongue.

It seemed probable that d'Albert had made the purchases Jens had reported. Krag at once sent Jens out to make inquiries, and he was back in half an hour quite out of breath. When he first had asked whether the goods had been sent to the "French gentleman," the shop-keeper had seemed quite surprised. But he admitted having sent various purchases to a Mr. d'Albert at the Victoria Hotel. Who had bought the goods, Jens next inquired. Then the shop-keeper had given so exact a description of d'Albert that it was absolutely certain he himself had bought the goods. Yet in this instance d'Albert had not spoken French. He had spoken Norwegian, and not only Norwegian, but the purest Christiania dialect. Not for a moment had the shop-keeper thought that his customer was anything but a Norwegian.

This was a valuable bit of news for Krag. Now he could put down on the credit column of his ledger that:

Mr. d'Albert, who hitherto has pretended to be a Frenchman knowing no other language, also spoke Norwegian, and the Norwegian of Christiania. And still more surprising was Jens' list of the articles which d'Albert had bought in this very ordinary second-hand clothing-place.

He had written everything down, and the list comprised: a pair of large seaman's boots, a pair of white wool socks, a pair of blue overalls, an Iceland wool-jacket—it had been sold for half-price as shop-worn, having grown dirty in the window—a plaid neckerchief and a brown sailor cap.

As soon as he glanced at the list Asbjörn Krag at once knew that Mr. d'Albert expected to disguise himself. Probably he wanted to go down to the docks. Had he begun to realize that he was being watched, and did he hope to make his escape aboard some ship, disguised as a sailor?

The detective did not think so. There were too

many proofs that some other plan was in the wind. It was now fifteen minutes past ten, and Mr. d'Albert had not as yet returned to the hotel. But Krag's faithful and omnipresent Jens had heard in the porter's box that d'Albert had ordered a closed auto for twelve o'clock sharp.

It was a foggy, rainy night, and extremely dark. Asbjörn Krag got into a disguise which was similar to that in which Mr. d'Albert evidently expected to appear that night. Krag always carried a suitcase containing various articles of clothing, so that he was in a position to change his outward appearance at a moment's notice.

And Jens, radiantly happy, also slipped into a pair of overalls which Krag had secured for him. When the two men looked at each other in the glass, they felt sure that they could easily be mistaken for a workman and his son.

Jens sneaked about d'Albert's room-door. From time to time he reported to Krag. The scientist was fussing around in his room with trunks and boots. Evidently he was changing his clothes.

Shortly before twelve d'Albert's closed automobile stopped in front of the hotel. Krag, too, had phoned for a car, and it already was parked on the opposite side of the street, at the hotel taxi stand. At twelve sharp Krag and his assistant left the hotel and got into their auto. Through the windows they

would be able to see the scientist enter his car. In
less than five minutes the hotel porter let out a gentleman who wore a long traveling coat and a cap.
It was d'Albert. Evidently the chauffeur had been
told where to drive, for the auto at once moved
away. Krag gave his own man the necessary instructions and then his car followed d'Albert's at
quite a distance, for Krag did not wish to let
d'Albert know that he was being followed. There
were now so few cars in the streets that Krag's
chauffeur had no difficulty in keeping the other car
in sight. Five seconds after the first car had turned
the corner the second followed it.

Krag had expected that d'Albert, in view of his
strange disguise, would not pass through the fine
residential quarter of Christiania, but would drive
directly down to the harbor. But what d'Albert did
was something quite different. He drove east,
through the most densely populated part of Christiania. Out on the eastern boundary of the city all
was dark and silent. The small wooden cottages
and the large tenements were all plunged in darkness. Not one of them showed a light, there was
not a sound except the grind of the rubber tires on
the stony road, and there was not a soul in sight.

At last the first auto stopped at the end of a street
which led directly to one of the great brickyards.
And not till then did it occur to Krag that the scien-

tist meant to meet some one in one of the yard
buildings.

If d'Albert was the leader of the band, what was
more likely than for him to have hidden away some
of his people in a brickyard after the police cap-
tures? The brickyards were places haunted by all
sorts of human flotsam and jetsam at night, vaga-
bonds of every kind, outcasts, men and women of
every age, people without shelter, who warmed
themselves around the great ovens in which the
bricks were baked. In such a crowd a couple of
men might disappear with ease.

Krag had his auto stopped at the corner. In company with Jens he got out and slowly drew near the
glowing lamps of the other car, which had stopped
in the darkness. As Krag and his companion passed
he heard some one beside the auto swearing and
cursing. It was a genuine Christiania voice. Krag
stepped up to the car. The chauffeur stood beside
the open door and was giving free rein to his rage.

"What's the matter?" asked the detective.

"He seems to have been blown away, the scoundrel!" shouted the chauffeur. "Here I've gone and
brought him to the end of the world, and now he
has made a get-away! I drove him once before, but
that time he did not sneak away on me!"

"Have you a lantern?"

The chauffeur had none.

So Krag threw the beam of his own pocket-lamp into the car. Its radiance lit every corner. And there, on the seat, lay the scientist's big mantle and ten ten-crown notes!

Eagerly the chauffeur snatched up the money and the mantle. He was now completely satisfied.

"He is a gentleman, after all!" he said. "Yes, I drove him once before. I know what he wants. He wants me to bring back his mantle to the hotel!"

"How often have you had him for a passenger?"

"Just once before this."

And the chauffeur closed the door and prepared to drive away.

"Where did you take him the other time?"

"Right to this very spot."

"And where did he go then?"

The chauffeur made no reply. After a moment he said: "Who are you, anyhow? You seem to have a good deal of curiosity in your system."

Krag let the light of his electric lamp play on the man's face, which evidently made him uncomfortable. Krag did not know him. But when the chauffeur saw Krag's silver police-shield shining in the light he groaned: "You are on the force? Well, I've done nothing out of the way!"

"Nobody says you did," answered Krag. "All I want is an answer to my question. Which way did he go?"

The chauffeur pointed to a little alley: "He went in there," he said.

"And how long did he stay?"

"Two full hours. When he came back dawn was breaking."

"Did you notice out of which house he came?"

"I don't think he came out of a house. He came across the fields."

Once more Krag thought of the brickyards.

"Was he alone?" he asked the chauffeur.

"Yes, he was all alone when he went, and when he came back. But when he came back he was reading a book."

"Was it light enough to read?" queried Krag.

"No, but he stopped under the street-light and read."

"Are you sure he was reading?"

"I am almost certain he was reading or writing. I saw the book."

Krag reflected a moment. It was plain there was no more to be discovered, and the man had disappeared. He had deceived Krag by one of the most everyday and elementary of tricks. He had jumped out of the auto while it was in motion and hidden from Krag's car, which had not yet turned the corner.

"You drove very slowly," said Krag. "Why did you do that?"

"The strange gentleman himself asked me to drive slow."

"When?"

"When he came out of the hotel."

"Did he make you drive slowly the other time?"

"No, that time I did not drive fast enough to suit him."

Then Krag knew that the scientist was aware, even before he had left the hotel, that he would be followed.

And now, in the darkness of night, any further attempt to track him would be useless. For the moment Krag had lost out. He could not enter the houses where every one was asleep and ask about a man dressed as a sailor. And there were so many brickyards on all sides that he would not have known which one to search first. There was nothing left to do but return to town.

Krag let the chauffeur drive on ahead with the empty car, and followed in the other with Jens.

Before they had gone very far a figure stepped out into the street and signaled Krag's car to stop.

"Is this auto No. 415?" asked the figure.

"Yes," replied Krag.

The unknown had moved into the light of the auto-lamps. He was a policeman.

"Not long ago you drove down the street in the opposite direction, did you not?" he asked.

"Yes."

"That's what I thought.   I saw your number by the street-light as you passed.   Did you know that you carried a passenger hanging on behind?"

"What?" cried Krag, eagerly.

"A full-grown man was hanging on to the rear end of your car."

"What did he look like?" asked Krag.

"He looked like a sailor."

"Confound it," cried Krag, "then we carried him there ourselves!"

CHAPTER IX

IT was two days after this strange event that the jewel-robber Thollon was arrested. And though Krag was very much taken up with his examination, he had also found time to keep in touch with matters at the hotel.

He had come to the conclusion that so many grounds of suspicion where the scientist was concerned had now developed, that he might venture to take a bolder stand without much risk.

At eleven o'clock in the forenoon d'Albert went out. Jens followed him and, a few minutes later, was able to inform Krag by telephone that Mr. d'Albert had gone to one of his scientific conferences with the eccentric scholar of Theater Street.

Then the whole case began to seem more like a fairy-tale than ever. Was d'Albert really the leader of the gang of criminals? Krag inclined more and more to the theory that he was. Yet in that case why did he keep on with his ridiculous pretext of ancient Egyptian studies? Was he really following some plan by so doing? Was he a genuine scholar or did he only want to bluff old Dr. Salinger? What was he up to in the dead of night out at the brickyards? And how had he managed to hang on to Krag's auto? That was not merely a trick, it was a very skillful piece of acrobatics.

As soon as Krag knew that d'Albert had arrived safely at Dr. Salinger's house, he determined to enter his room at the hotel, something he thus far had not ventured to do.

It was, of course, not hard for him to open the room-door with a skeleton key. He took care, however, that no one should see him, and carefully locked the door again as soon as he was in the room.

And as he stood in d'Albert's room for the very first time he noticed that he felt slightly nervous. If he was mistaken, then he had committed a very serious blunder. Yet if his conclusions were correct, he stood on the threshold of important discoveries.

The room looked like any other hotel room, but the immaculate order which reigned in it at once struck the eye. A large American trunk stood on a trunk-stand in one corner. On it were pasted a number of labels, among them the labels of hotels in Nice, Cairo and Paris. Krag tried to open it with his skeleton key, but in vain. In the clothing closet, very carefully hung up, were various suits—evening dress, walking suits, smoking jackets—and a bath-robe lay folded across the back of a chair.

With much interest Krag looked for the sailor clothes of the preceding night, but they were

nowhere to be seen. Very likely d'Albert had ex-
changed them this very day for other things. But
where had he been? Had he visited one of his
fellow-gangsters? Had he gone to one of his
"stations"?

Arranged on the broad window-ledge was a long
row of thick, bound books. Krag could read their
titles. They were all scientific works dealing with
Egyptian philology, religion and culture.

Krag moved around the room with the greatest
care. He glided about like a cat. He did not wish
to cause the slightest disorder, for he knew that the
mysterious scholar was gifted with extraordinarily
keen powers of observation, and would at once notice
the slightest change.

The drawers of the writing-desk were locked.
New locks had been put in, something which, incidentally, Krag already had been told by the hotel
porter. The detective did not even make an attempt
to open them; he knew they would not yield to his
skeleton key.

But he did look with a great deal of interest at a
bulky manuscript which lay wide open on the table.
It was written in French, and the author had
reached page 1614. Krag turned over the manuscript pages. The title-page indicated that it was
a treatise dealing with a certain period of Egyptian
history. Many hieroglyphics occurred in the text.

And then the detective noticed something that roused his astonishment in the highest degree.

Under a leaden paperweight he found three memorandum slips torn from an ordinary yellow note-pad. And on each page was written a sentence in Norwegian. On the first was written: "Bamboo grows in the shade." On the second: "Hole in the corner." And on the third: "He has ink on his fingers."

This last expression in particular, from the dialect of Christiania's underworld, seemed so funny to the detective that he could not help but chuckle softly as he read it.

He read and reread the three mysterious sentences. Then he carefully studied the hand-writing. The sentences had been written with lead-pencil and the letters were traced with a very uncertain hand. He could not help thinking of the chauffeur's remark that the mysterious scholar, when he had come back from the neighborhood of the brickyards, had been reading or writing.

Krag knew what all three expressions meant. They were slang phrases used by the Christiania criminal world. In spite of their apparent lack of meaning, they meant a good deal to anyone who understood the language of yegg-men and house-breakers. Two of the expressions were communications which must have been of great importance, at the moment, for the persons who were supposed to read them. The third was an order.

The expression "Bamboo grows in the shade" merely meant that the police were on the trail. This was a warning. "Look out for yourself, the police are after you, though you do not see them."

"He has ink on his fingers" was another communication. This characteristic slang phrase of the criminal underworld meant that the person in question already had been convicted of some crime. The expression probably came from the finger-print process, for the finger-prints of every criminal were registered in the Berthillon department. And among his comrades, they say of a man whose finger-prints have been taken, "has ink on his fingers."

But the expression "Hole in the corner" was the most mysterious of all to any man who did not know thieves' slang. In spite of its brevity, it was full of meaning. It expressed at the same time an order, a threat and a warning. It meant that danger was near, and that would be necessary to think of making an escape. Asbjörn Krag now thought it possible that one or more of the leader's gang had discovered that their master was being shadowed. Perhaps they had found out that Krag lived beneath the same roof and in the next room. And in thieves' slang the situation was expressed by saying that the person in question was in a "corner" formed by the police, that he was surrounded. So when he got the notice "Hole in the corner" it meant that he must by all means try to escape, since the eleventh hour for a getaway had arrived.

Once he had read these three communications, Krag no longer had the least doubt but that Mr. d'Albert belonged to a well-organized gang of criminals and, in all probability, was their leader. On the other hand, it was not at all clear to him whether Mr. d'Albert had *received* the three notices or meant to *send* them out.

For the moment he contented himself with making note of them, and then continued his investigations.

The only thing in the room which was open was d'Albert's hand-bag of toilet articles. And it was plain that only pure forgetfulness on the scholar's part was responsible for the fact. All his other things had been put under lock and key with the caution one might expect a diplomat—or a burglar— to show.

This hand-bag looked exactly like the one which had disappeared from the Hotel Malmo, and had belonged to Thollon's master. It was filled with costly and elegant toilet articles. Its contents, like everything else in the room, betrayed a wealthy, distinguished traveler.

Among the toilet articles Krag found two things

which interested him especially—a white peruque
and a pair of grey side-whiskers. As he held them
in his hand a vague recollection rose in his mind.
Where had he seen this hair and these Dundrearies?

He could not at once place the recollection. So
he walked over to the mirror and put on the peruque.
And the recollection grew stronger. But where,
where had he seen such a man?

Now he fastened on the Dundrearies. And when
he looked at himself in the glass he suddenly knew
where he had seen this disguise before.

It was at Consul Birger's poker-evening.

It was the disguise worn by the servant, the counterfeit Jean, who had stolen all the cardplayers'
money with such unexampled cleverness.

Krag looked at his watch. He dared not prolong
his stay in the room. So he put back the things in
the trunk, just as he had found them, and left the
room, locking the door behind him.

. . . .

Krag had another curious experience that same
day, before the ensuing night and the morning which
followed brought a decisive event. This other incident also took place in the Victoria Hotel, and made
the detective's position much more difficult, because
it totally upset some of the conclusions at which he
had arrived.

Mr. d'Albert returned to the hotel at four o'clock

sharp. He was dressed like any other gentleman, and seemed to have come from breakfast in town. He wore a white rose in his button-hole. This frivolous flower was in striking contrast to his serious, scholarly features. Krag at once weighed the possibility that d'Albert might be wearing the rose as a signal of some sort.

D'Albert went straight up to his room and remained there for half an hour. At first Krag heard him walking restlessly up and down, as though in deep thought. Then everything became quiet. At last he came out, carefully locked his door, and went down to the dining-room, where he ordered tea and sat reading the newspapers. After that he went to the telephone-booth. Krag could not find out to whom he had phoned, but it must have been a local call.

Naturally, while his suspect was doing all these every-day things the detective's tension increased. There was something in the air. The silence in the hotel corridors, d'Albert's present calm were in striking contrast to his restless activity in his own room. Whether a catastrophe or merely the solution of the riddle impended, it was plain that something was about to occur.

D'Albert returned to his room, and soon Jens reported that he was fussing about with his trunks and his clothes. Jens could not see, but he could hear the mysterious scholar opening and shutting trunks, taking off his shoes and so forth.

Krag at once jumped to the conclusion that d'Albert was about to disguise himself once more. A few minutes later Jens again came to him and reported that not a sound was audible in d'Albert's room, and that he thought the latter must have left it a few minutes before. Krag hurried out into the hall. Peeping through the keyhole he could make out a light burning in the room. Hence there was no key in the door: d'Albert must have gone.

Krag hurried to the porter's lodge.

Ahead of him, in the long hall, he saw a figure which looked familiar to him. It was that of a smallish, gray-haired man, who wore a pair of gray Dundrearies. And suddenly as he realized who it was, the detective experienced a feeling of great satisfaction.

He really believed that at last he was on the point of solving all the mysteries, and that he could take the step which, for the past few days, had been the end and aim of all his striving: d'Albert's arrest.

The figure in front of him, moving along with a heavy and measured tread, could be none other than that of the mysterious scholar.

Now Krag realized why Jens had heard such curious noises proceeding from d'Albert's room: the latter had been disguising himself.

An amusing memory passed through Krag's mind: it was the recollection of the evening at Consul Birger's, when the poker-players' money had been stolen.

Krag remembered how on that evening the daring thief had played the rôle of Birger's servant, and thus secured an opportunity to pick the pockets of the guests.

He also recalled that, only a few hours before, when he had searched the Egyptologist's room, he had been very much surprised to discover the wig and whiskers in the open hand-bag, and how remarkably they resembled the hair and sideboards of Birger's old servant. It had at once made clear that d'Albert must have been the thief on the night in question.

And now, at last, he had proof, incontestable proof that this was the case.

Mr. d'Albert, criminal and Egyptologist, was setting out on some new enterprise, and had thought it best once more to assume the disguise of the old servant.

While Krag followed the figure in front of him, these reflections passing through his mind, he could not help but admire the remarkable skill the man displayed in his disguises. As the latter now walked along the hall he was the old servant, Jean, in every least little detail. Krag admitted to himself that

d'Albert's impersonation was a masterly bit of acting. He already looked forward with pleasure to
taking hold of him and arresting him.

Under his arm the old man carried a small box.
It looked like a razor-case or a jewel-case. Krag
suspected that this little case hid a secret: his fingers
itched to snatch it. But first he wanted to let the
man reach the porter's lodge, for he wanted wit-
nesses when he unmasked the robber.

When pursued and pursuer drew near the porter's
lodge Krag stepped up to the servant and said in
French: "Just a moment, I should like to speak to
you!" At the same time he beckoned to the hotel
porter, and the latter, somewhat surprised, stepped
up. Krag then seized the servant's right arm and
held it. At that moment the servant turned around
and—Krag was looking into eyes really dim with
age!

For a moment the detective was nonplussed as he
looked into those eyes. "My God," he thought,
"can the fellow disguise his soul as well as his body?
Those are not d'Albert's eyes! . . ."

"I do not understand you," said the servant, in
Norwegian, "what do you mean?"

"We can talk Norwegian, if you prefer," answered Krag, and took a firmer grip on his arm,
"but why not drop your play-acting?"

The old man's eyes opened wide. "Play-acting?"

he murmured. "What do you want of me? I am an old man. I have done nothing wrong!"

Krag clutched the gray Dundrearies firmly in his hand. "Off with those false whiskers!" he said.

And then everything turned dark before his eyes —for the servant uttered a genuine cry of pain. His Dundrearies did not come off. His whiskers were *real!*

Suddenly Krag tore the little case from the old fellow's hand and opened it. It contained pearls, a wonderful collection of the finest pearls.

Krag felt greatly relieved when he saw the jewels. Not for a moment did he dream they were anything but the proceeds of some robbery.

Meanwhile the old man stood and wailed: "My master's jewels!"

Krag looked at him and—he could not help himself—he had to take hold of his hair and pull it. But the old man's hair grew on his head; it was just as real as his Dundrearies.

Now the old fellow was quite pale with anger and pain. He was about to call out but suddenly stopped, with his eyes fixed on the detective's face.

An expression of recognition and of the greatest surprise showed on his features.

"Ah, now I know who you are!" he cried. "You were one of my master's guests. It was on that terrible evening! . . ."

In that moment of disappointment the realization of his mistake swept over Krag's brain like a devouring fire. He quickly drew the old man into an adjoining room and motioned the porter to leave him.

So it really was the old servant Jean and not d'Albert in disguise.

"What are you doing here in the hotel?"

"I had a commission to carry out for my master."

"With these pearls? What did you want to do with them?"

"I came to get them."

"From whom?"

"From the gentleman in room No. 24, Mr. d'Albert. He is one of my master's friends."

"How did the pearls happen to get into Mr. d'Albert's hands?"

"He was to examine them. They are Corinthian pearls, and during the past few years have lost much of their lustre. Mr. d'Albert is a specialist in jewels, and they were given him to examine. He claims that sick pearls can be treated and made well again. He himself is a collector of fine pearls."

Krag glanced critically at the pearls. They were genuine beyond the shadow of a doubt. He returned the jewel-case to the servant.

"The whole thing is a misunderstanding," he said, "but we are obliged to keep an eye open here at the

hotel, for during the season, when it is full of trav-
elers, jewel robberies often happen."

The servant went off with the jewels, somewhat
confused and very much surprised; while Krag returned to his room. In the hall he met Mr. d'Albert,
who was about to go out. Mr. d'Albert smiled. It
was the first time that Krag had ever seen him smile.

CHAPTER X

THE THEFT OF THE DECORATION

WHEN Krag returned to his room after his unfortunate encounter with the old servant, he really felt like a beaten man.

To all appearances the whole incident was of secondary importance, and the old servant's turning up might have had nothing whatever to do with the rest of the strange case, yet, somehow, Krag could not help but look on the whole thing as a direct insult to himself.

And when he reviewed the happening more in detail two facts made him shake his head.

First of all, there was the strange coincidence that Consul Birger's servant was in the hotel, almost immediately after he, Krag, had discovered the disguise—the wig and false whiskers—in d'Albert's room. Secondly, there was Mr. d'Albert's telephone call.

When he put together these two facts they pointed to a solution which dumbfounded him, because they showed a cunning and shrewdness on d'Albert's part such as Krag never before had encountered in his whole career.

And the probability that Mr. d'Albert, on his

return to his room, had noticed that it had been searched, supplied the connecting link between the two facts.

It is true that Krag had put back everything he had examined exactly in its place, but notwithstanding the greatest care, he would have to take for granted that d'Albert's keen eyes had remarked a change.

What had been the scholar's thoughts in that event? That he was discovered? And what would be the first thing that would occur to him? He must discount the discovery and forestall its possible consequences. And he had done so by telephoning Consul Birger that he could send his servant for the pearls which he, d'Albert, had been given to test.

He knew that as soon as Krag saw a man of old Jean's appearance turn up in the hotel, he would make some false move or, at any rate, be very much confused. Both expectations had been fully realized.

First of all Krag had made a false move. Furthermore, his deductions had been completely upset. And in addition d'Albert had been treated to some moments of genuine amusement, which brought a smile to his usually serious and scholarly face. Krag realized that he had been beaten, horse, foot and dragoons, in the little skirmish.

Very much dissatisfied, he returned to his house. He was dissatisfied with himself, dissatisfied with the general situation, dissatisfied with everybody and everything. He already had several sleepless nights behind him, but he had not made the slightest progress. And yet—all the time he had the disagreeable feeling that there was something going on, that the darkness about him was full of evil activity, and that at any moment something might explode.

He did not fall asleep until around one o'clock and when he woke up the morning sun was streaming in at his window. He looked at his watch. It was eight o'clock. He felt remarkably nervous, something very unusual with him after a good night's sleep.

He rang for his landlady and had her fetch him his morning coffee and the papers. With feverish haste he turned their pages with a strange, indefinite feeling that something must have happened. But all he saw were the usual articles, items of daily news, foreign telegrams, and so forth.

But a few minutes after he had left his tub there was a violent ring at his room-door.

He listened: first he head his housekeeper's frightened voice, and then a grumbling voice replying to it.

He could not make out what was said, but caught the word "telephone."

A moment later the speaker stood in the room.

He was an officer from police headquarters, and

was about to deliver his message with breathless haste, when Krag forestalled him.

"Before you tell me anything," said Krag, "I should like to know why you came here in person instead of telephoning?"

"We could not get you on the phone," said the officer, "the wire must have been cut."

"Very well," said Krag, "then get your news off your chest. Has some new mysterious robbery been committed, or is it a terrible crime?"

"Yes," answered the officer, "this time a terrible crime has been committed."

Krag was startled by the man's tragic face and asked in alarm: "You don't mean to tell me it is a matter of life and death?"

"No."

"Well then, what is it?"

"The Italian," said the police officer, "the Italian broke jail last night!"

Asbjörn Krag stood as though frozen fast to the ground. This almost unbelievable news had given him a severe shock. If true, it might mean beginning all over again.

He looked at the man and he must have seemed incredulous, for the officer stammered: "It's the truth! He escaped last night!"

"And the rest," asked Krag, "did they make their getaway too?"

"No," answered the officer, "that red-haired waiter and Thollon are still in jail."

"But how did the Italian escape?"

"He opened the door of his cell."

Krag smiled. "Can you open a cell-door from the inside?" he asked.

"No, of course not. The whole thing is a mystery. But it clear that the door was opened."

"Was it blown open?"

"No, there was no trace of violence. The door was simply opened, and that is all there is to it. Yes, I know it sounds strange, but I am telling you nothing but the truth."

"When did it happen?"

"It must have happened after the second patrol, about half-past four in the morning."

Again Krag smiled. "All right, I'll grant you the door," he said. "But how could the man get through the hall of the jail corridor, down the stairs, and out of the main entrance?"

"That is what we can't find out. He has not left the slightest clue. And no one heard or saw anything. The investigation is under way now, and I was sent to get you."

Krag reflected for a moment. "You remember the Italian's examination, don't you?"

"Yes."

"Do you remember the threats he made?"

The officer looked Krag directly in the eye:

"I remember one of them," he said.

"And which was that?"

"He threatened to make his escape from jail inside of three days."

"Well, he made good his words. And then?"

"Then he said as soon as he was free he would commit a robbery in your own home."

"Quite right. And what was he going to steal?"

"He was going to steal your decoration, the cross of the order with which you have been decorated."

"Right! And do you remember where I am supposed to keep my cross?"

"In your writing-desk, in the lower left-hand drawer."

Krag nodded.

"That is all quite correct," he said, "and do you really think the man has carried out his threat?"

"I think it quite possible."

Asbjörn Krag took his head in both his hands.

"Do you feel ill?" asked the officer. "You look very pale!"

"No doubt you are right," Krag answered. "My head feels unusually heavy. I must have slept longer last night than was good for me. I did not wake up until eight o'clock.

"Your hands are trembling!"

Krag stretched out his hands. His fingertips were

moving nervously up and down.

"That's funny," he said as he looked at them. "I feel as though I had taken a dose of morphine. And yet I have taken no morphine for over a month."

Then he went to his desk. He beckoned to the officer. "Come over here a moment!"

Krag shook out his keys until he found the right one. Then he put it in the lock.

"This is the lower left-hand drawer," he remarked. "All I want to say before I open it is that yesterday afternoon my cross was here in its place."

He opened the drawer. The cross of the order had disappeared!

As though stricken with paralysis, both men stood in front of the deck. There was no possible doubt. The daring pickpocket had carried out his threat and had carried it out successfully.

He had broken jail, had paid Krag a visit during the night, and had stolen his decoration.

Krag trembled in every limb. Again and again his mind returned to the thought that the thief a few hours past, while he was sleeping, had been so close to him that he could have touched him had he stretched out his hand.

Krag had been in danger of losing his life.

And yet the robber had not taken advantage of the opportunity.

It seemed characteristic of this strange gang of criminals that they were really "friendly" where their victims were concerned. They enjoyed robbing them, teasing them, threatening them, but did them no real injury. All in all, they were an amiable band, and once more Krag, standing before the rifled drawer, was obliged to admit that they had a sense of humor. It was plain that some of the gang's members would run any risk for the sake of a good joke.

But now it occurred to Krag how strange it was that he had slept through the burglar's visit. Ordinarily he was a light sleeper, the slightest sound awakened him. And why was his head so heavy? There was a strange buzzing in his ears which seemed to indicate that his nervous system was out of order.

He rang for his landlady, and had her bring some of the milk and remains of his supper the preceding evening.

A rapid investigation in his laboratory proved that there was no suspicious substance in the milk, but that a large quantity of veronal had been mixed with the salt.

Now everything was clear to him. He had been drugged.

His landlady told him that only the day before she had sent for the table salt together with other things to the neighboring grocery store where she made all her purchases.

Krag sent for the boy who had fetched the groceries home for the landlady. He told a curious tale. After he had bought the groceries and was on his way back to Krag's house, a man without a hat, who said he was the grocer's assistant, had run after\ him and called out that he had taken the wrong things. The man asked the boy to let him look in the basket. He went through the basket and checked up the purchases. No, everything was all right, after all, the grocer's assistant said, after he had finished checking up, and he apologized for his mistake. The boy did not see anything strange about the incident, and took home the groceries without saying anything to the landlady about it.

So now Krag knew why he had slept so long and so soundly. Now he realized what admirable plans, carefully considered down to the very last detail, the daring gang was capable of hatching and carrying out.

Then he made a rapid examination of the house. A close testing of the various locks showed how the thief had gone to work. First he had opened the house-door with an ordinary key. Then he had gone into the court and broken out one of the window-panes, after having rubbed it in with soap. After that the man reached the kitchen stairs by climbing through the broken window, had opened the kitchen door with a skeleton key, and had passed through the other rooms to Krag's bed-room.

The most mysterious point was the lock of the writing-desk. Though it was a lock of a most peculiar and intricate pattern, there was not the slightest traces of violence. In some way or other the thief must have gotten hold of a key which fitted it.

It took Krag a quarter-of-an-hour to gather these facts. And not until then did he consent to accompany the officer to police headquarters.

The police auto was waiting in front of the house and both men got in and drove off.

The unusual restlessness shown at police headquarters made it clear that something out of the ordinary had taken place.

Policemen in uniform and detectives in plain clothes were hurrying around all over the building.

In the Chief of Police's office Krag found one of the scrub-women of the jail under examination. Krag smiled when he saw the woman. With tears streaming down her cheeks she stood in front of the Chief of Police, and stammered again and again that she was as innocent as a babe unborn. It was not her fault, she said, she could not help it, she had been ill-treated herself, and so forth and so on.

The Chief of Police stamped his foot impatiently.

"That's just what I keep telling you," he said. "You may not have done so purposely, but you helped the man escape just the same!"

"Can't you explain it to us,?' asked Krag, seating himself in front of the woman and looking at her.

"It was yesterday evening," she began, sobbing.

The Chief interrupted her: "Your explanation does not hang together at all. But still it has given me a vague glimmering of what happened."

Krag looked at him.

"Do you remember that idiot jewel-thief?" asked the Chief of Police. Heaven be praised, we still have him, at any rate! You were right—he was not nearly as idiotic as he seemed to be. And then we have the red-haired waiter."

Krag smiled and nodded his head.

"We owe it to Mr. Thollon that Ferro was informed. Thollon must have given the Italian some secret signals when the two were confronted, just as you suspected. Otherwise I do not see how Ferro could have been so well informed. For he knew all he needed to know. This morning, at five o'clock, he was in his cell, all ready to escape. He knew what would happen and only Thollen could have given him the information."

"I was quite certain of that in my own mind when the two men were confronted," said Krag, "that Thollon passed on a communication to Ferro."

"Well, then," the Chief of Police continued, "now this poor woman tells me that yesterday evening a strange man stepped up to her and offered her twenty crowns if she would go along with him and clean up his apartment at once, for it had to be done right away.   She is one of the scrub-women for the jail.   She cleans it out and comes to work every morning at five with her mop and pail.

Krag smiled and nodded as though he already knew what had happened.

"Of course she went along with the stranger," the Chief of Police continued, "and he took her to a house in Water Street.   There the people first had her sit down and drink a cup of coffee.   And it is hardly necessary to mention that from the moment she drank the coffee until she woke up this morning at eight o'clock, she remembered nothing at all."

"Quit right," Krag added, "and it is unnecessary to mention that another person disguised as a scrub-woman appeared in jail in her place."

Here the scrub-woman broke out into a desperate fit of sobbing, and it took some time before she was soothed and quieted.

The police officials and detectives who were gathered in the police headquarters rooms did not for a moment suspect that at this very moment a stranger was ascending the broad flight of steps which led to the main entrance.

This stranger, evidently a foreigner, carried a large brief-case under his arm. He evidently was in a great hurry.

He was quite a young man. He did not look like Ferro, or the stupid jewel-thief, or the learned Mr. d'Albert. The dust of travel still clung to his clothes. Evidently he had just stepped from a train.

And it was this man who was to supply the solution of the whole mystery. It was a solution totally unsuspected by any of the police authorities. It was a solution unsuspected even by Asbjörn Krag.

CHAPTER XI

BUT before the stranger had forced his way through the crowd in the great anteroom of the police headquarters building, in order to reach the room where the officials who had the case in hand and who knew nothing of his arrival, were busy, the investigation of Ferro's escape had been concluded.

The scrub-woman had been drugged and held a prisoner in Water Street. Meanwhile one of the gang had taken possession of her tools, her pail, her mop and brushes, and the next morning, shortly before five o'clock, had turned up at police headquarters.

The rascal who played her rôle had shown remarkable skill in disguising himself as a scrub-woman, and the patrolman on duty did not hesitate a moment to let him in. For a time the counterfeit scrub-woman fussed about in the hall with her pail and mop, but when one of the other scrub-women began to talk to her and showed signs of entering into a conversation, she had a sudden coughing spell, and went off along one of the prison corridors.

It was the very day on which the prison-floor was

scrubbed. The gangster masquerading as a scrub-woman must have known where Ferro's cell was located. By means of a clever mechanism which enabled the possessor to open solid door-locks, he managed to get into Ferro's cell.

Under his disguise he had a scrub-woman's complete outfit. The Italian put on these clothes, and winding a large handkerchief which hid half his face around his head, he and his rescuer mingled with the rest of the scrub-women, and went through all the motions of hard work with their pails and mops.

The exact hour when the two criminals escaped out of the police department building could not be fixed. But that they had not excited the least attention in their disguise was plainly shown by the results: both had escaped without leaving a trace.

"And now we are just about where we started," said the Chief of Police. "It is true we still have the red-haired waiter and the idiotic jewel-thief, but we can't get anything out of them."

"But we have other things to go by," said Krag.

"Which?" asked the Chief of Police.

"First of all we have the traces left by the thief who visited me. They may be useful once I have had time to make a more detailed investigation. Then there is the house in Water Street where the scrub-woman was kept a prisoner. Who rented it?

What did the man who engaged it look like? Where did he hail from? Finally, we have the counterfeit scrub-woman. How did she manage to secure the right one's mop and pail? Did any one catch sight of her? And how did the two disguised scrub-women pass through the streets? Did no one notice them?"

"All these things may lead to results if we combine them with facts already known to us."

"But what do we really know, if it comes to that?" asked the Chief of Police with an anger which may readily be understood.

"We know," answered Krag, "that the leader of this gang is still here in town, in Christiania. I even think that I have seen and have spoken to him."

"And you did not arrest him?"

"No."

"Why not?"

"It is possible that I am mistaken," replied Krag, "and this possibility is a very dangerous one. I can only make an arrest when I am positively convinced I am right. But I may meet the gentleman in question again any minute. He cannot take a step in any direction without my being at once informed of his movements."

A long painful silence now settled down on all present. Every one felt that the whole situation was nearing a point where it threatened to become out and out ridiculous.

At last the Chief of Police said: "It seems to me that we are dealing with people who do nothing but make fools of us! I have a distinct, unpleasant feeling that we are not dealing with real criminals."

"There you are taking a step nearer the actual truth," Krag answered. "I am positively convinced that we are not dealing with professional criminals in the ordinary sense."

Again there was a long pause.

"But what are we to do with the red-haired waiter and Thollon?" the Chief of Police suddenly asked.

Krag turned to him with a smile: "Turn them loose," he said.

"Turn them loose? What do you mean? Then we will not have a single member of the gang in our power."

"My idea," said Krag, "is that if we turn them loose it is possible that they will enable us to secure what we cannot secure if they are kept in jail."

"And what is that?"

"They may lead us to the gang's real hiding-place. Turn them both loose and I guarantee that they will not again escape observation. From the moment they walk down the steps of this building every move they make will be watched. And at the same time they must not be worried. Their suspicions must be lulled until they feel it is quite safe to hunt up the gang's place of refuge. You must admit that this plan is one that holds forth a good chance of success. At any rate, we will get nothing from either of them as long as they locked up."

The Chief of Police shook his head dubiously as Krag disclosed his plan. He thought that the police had already lost so much prestige in the matter that they could not risk losing the last pawns they held.

But at the very moment when he was putting this thought into words, an attendant reported that a strange gentleman, evidently a foreigner, begged for an interview with the Chief of Police regarding a matter which brooked no delay.

It was the man in traveling clothes who a few minutes before had ascended the stairs of the police building in such haste.

"What does he want to see me about?" asked the Chief of Police.

"He spoke French," said the attendant. "So far as I could make out he wished to tell the police something about the matter in which they were most interested at this very moment."

The officials in the room looked at one another.

"Show him in," said the Chief of Police. And the attendant disappeared, while the still weeping scrub-woman was led out of the room by two policemen.

The Chief of Police and Krag were left alone.

Krag rose. Both men's eyes were fixed on the door.

"Nothing surprises me any more," said Krag, suddenly.

"What do you mean?" the Chief asked.

"I would not be surprised if in another minute we were to stand face to face with the leader of the gang!"

The Chief of Police started. "Do you think he really would have the impudence . . ."

The door opened. The foreign gentleman appeared on the threshold. He was a tall lean man, typically southern in his features and appearance.

"No, it is not he," said Krag.

"Have I the honor of addressing the Chief of Police of Christiania?" the stranger asked.

The Chief of Police introduced himself.

The stranger bowed to Asbjôrn Krag. "And this, perhaps, is the gentleman who sent a telegram to the fifth division of the Paris police, regarding a certain Egyptologist, a Mr. d'Albert?"

Krag opened his eyes. "I am the sender of the telegram," he said.

The polite stranger bowed once more. "I am glad to hear it," he said. "My name is Chevillard and I am the Egyptologist's lawyer."

"Then the Egyptologist really exists?" queried Krag.

"Yes, and at this moment is in Christiania."

The stranger was asked to seat himself and did so, putting down his brief-case on the table before him with a gesture full of meaning.

"I take for granted," he began, "that you gentlemen have been confronted with a series of strange crimes?"

Krag nodded.   "Such is the case," he said.

The stranger's face showed unmistakable signs of distress.

"Before I continue," he remarked, "I should like to know the nature of these offences. I take for granted, first of all, that they have been property crimes, larcenies."

"Yes."

"House-breaking?"

"Yes."

"Forgery?"

"That also."

"Cheating at play?"

"Possibly."

"Attacks on individuals?"

"Yes."

The stranger hesitated a moment and then in a low tone of voice said:

"Murder?"

"No," replied Krag.

The stranger uttered a sigh of relief.

"Heaven be praised, that the crimes are only larcencies and robberies! How much does their sum total amount to? A hundred thousand crowns?"

"Fully that amount."

"There will be no difficulty regarding that," said the stranger.

He opened his brief-case and drew from it an oblong strip of paper.

"Before I say another word," he remarked, "I will ask you to examine this scrap of paper. I am sure it will lend greater weight to what I am about to tell you."

The bit of paper was a check on the *Credit Lyonnaise,* one of the greatest Paris Banking-houses, for two hundred thousand francs.

The two police officials, dumbfounded, first stared at the stranger who called himself Chevillard, and claimed to be d'Albert's lawyer, and then at each other.

The lawyer said no more. He was enjoying the little triumph which the production of the check had given him. After both the Chief and Krag had examined the check they laid it down on the table again. It was a certified check, evidently genuine. If presented that very moment at the Central Office of the Bank of Norway in Christiania, the sum of two hundred thousand francs would at once be paid to the bearer.

But what did it all mean?

The Chief of Police was altogether at a loss. The whole affair already had taken on a development to which he was unaccustomed. And here came a brand-new man and said: "I am this daring bandit-leader's lawyer. My name is so and so. Here is a check for two hundred thousand francs. It is my intention to come to terms with you gentlemen!"

The Chief looked at Krag in order to get an idea of what the detective thought from his expression.

But to tell the truth, Asbjörn Krag himself was greatly confused.

His very first thought was: Is the appearance of this mysterious stranger a new move in the gang's campaign? Is it the signal for fresh attacks? Is it a daring attempt of some kind?

But what could be the object of another attack?

Krag subjected the man to a close examination.

No, beyond any doubt, the man really had been traveling. He really had been riding in a railroad coach.

Krag asked: "Did you just arrive in town?"

The question seemed to surprise the stranger: "Yes," he replied, "I arrived by train, half-an-hour ago. I registered at a hotel without losing a minute. But I am sure you will excuse me for not having washed and brushed up before coming here. I felt that it was urgently necessary for me to see you at once."

"You were quite right," Krag answered, "the matter is very urgent. But if you have just left the train, no doubt you still have your return drawing-room ticket about you.

The stranger at once put his hand in his pocket and produced it: Christiania to Paris. Krag gave the stamp only a single glance. It was in perfect order.

Then the stranger realized why Asbjörn Krag had asked for his ticket. He took from his briefcase various papers which he spread out before the two officials.

"I can readily understand," he said, "especially in this affair, that you gentlemen wish to know with whom you are dealing. Here is my license as a member of the Paris Bar. Here is my personal card and, better yet, my passport, viséed by the Minister of Foreign Affairs only two days ago. In addition I can offer you a special letter of recommendation from the Norwegian Embassy in Paris."

Krag read this last document with the greatest interest. In it the ambassador stated that the bearer was one of the best-known lawyers in the city of Paris, and had gone to Christiania on a special mission. On the result of his mission, the ambassador added, depended whether certain highly respected and distinguished families would or would not be entangled in a catastrophe due to no fault of theirs.

When the Chief of Police also had examined the papers he said: "In view of what you have shown us we cannot well refuse to negotiate with you. Your papers are entirely satisfactory."

Mr. Chevillard nodded.

"Well, then," he said, "let us get to work. I hope that nothing has happened which cannot be straigtened out. As you may imagine, my appearance here in Christiania has a disturbing reason behind it. But first of all, tell me what has taken place in your city?"

"Is it your intention to question us regarding the mysterious crimes which have caused us so much astonishment and apprehension during the past few months?"

"To judge by the telegram which Mr. Asbjörn Krag sent the Paris police, I take for granted that a certain individual, a Frenchman by the name of d'Albert, has been living in Christiania for some time."

When Asbjörn Krag heard this name he gave a sigh of relief. After all, and it was a satisfaction to know it, his suspicions regarding the mysterious scholar at the Victoria Hotel had obviously been well founded.

"You are right," he said. "This Frenchman has caused us a great deal of trouble lately. He has committed a series of startling crimes in our town, and carried them out with the most unheard of impudence and daring."

"In spite of that I feel relieved," replied the lawyer, "to think that murder has not been done!"

"Can you give me some information concerning this person?" asked Krag.

"Yes. For the moment I will merely say that he is a genius—not only as a criminal, but in other fields as well."

"That is very probable. Is he really a Frenchman?"

"Yes."

"For a time I thought he must be a Norwegian."

"Because the Norwegian he speaks is so perfect, isn't that it?"

"Absolutely."

"A Persian would say the same thing. Or a Greek, or a Portuguese. He is one of the greatest linguists in the world. Not only does he speak all languages but he speaks all the dialects of every language."

"Is it true that he is a distinguished Egyptologist?"

"Absolutely true. I take for granted that here in Christiania he has studied everything in the way of Egyptian antiquities to be found in your museums."

"Yes, he has."

There was a pause. Then the lawyer said: "I

suppose it is hardly necessary for me to mention that I have come to Christiania to save this man."

"To save him?" said the Chief of Police with a smile. "He has committed a number of criminal violations of the law. I can assure you that his punishment will be correspondingly severe."

"And I assure you that this man must not be punished!"

Asbjörn Krag now took a hand in the conversation.

"In order to punish him," he said, "he first has to be arrested. Since this gentleman has informed us that the Mr. d'Albert living at the Victoria Hotel is identical with the criminal we are seeking, it seems as though the moment to arrest him has arrived."

But the lawyer stretched out a warning hand.

"That will not help you," he said. "You may feel sure that the gentleman in question knows of my presence in Christiania this very moment. You may be sure that he already had taken into consideration the possibility that you may try to lay hands on him without listening to me."

"How should he know that you are here?"

The lawyer smiled. "In the simplest way in the world, because I informed him. He is my client, you know."

"It will be time enough to defend him when he is brought into court. He will be taken before a Nor-

wegian court, and the court will assign a Norwegian
lawyer to defend him.

The Chief of Police happened to glance at the
check lying on the table and his face twitched.

The stranger noticed it and said: "Do not misunderstand me. This money is to be used to make
good any damage Mr. d'Albert may have done. If
this sum is not sufficient, there is more money avail-
able. Mr. d'Albert is not only a great scholar. He
also is a multi-millionaire. He is a multi-millionaire
and—a thief, gentleman! Perhaps you may have
suspected that it was the study of the Egyptian hieroglyphics which made him the world's master pickpocket."

"No," said Krag, "I must confess I fail to see the
connection."

"I will admit," continued the French lawyer, "that
this must sound like a strange contradiction of terms.
Yet I am convinced that you will see the connection
once I tell you the story of this strange and distinguished personality. I take for granted that what
surprises you most is the lack of proportion between
his position as multi-millionaire and his position as a
master-thief."

"No, at bottom this is not so strange," Krag answered, as he began to gather up and glance over the
papers scattered about the table. "If your client has
worked as successfully in other capitals as he has in

Christiania, I can understand how he laid the foundation of his fortune."

"You are entirely mistaken, my dear sir. My client has done nothing but lose money in all his thefts. I can assure you that such is the case from my personal knowledge."

"But in that event it seems very strange that he does not give up his criminal career," said the Chief of Police. "At any rate, it does not seem as though he had suffered any losses in connection with his thefts here in Christiania. Will you be good enough to read the list, Mr. Krag!"

"Yes, I should be greatly interested in hearing it," said the lawyer, taking out a memorandum-book, "for then I can put down the sums to be made good more in detail." And he added, wearily: "I do not mind saying that this is not the first time I have had to make similar computations."

"Well, then, you shall know what the great Egyptologist has been doing here in Christiania. I cannot believe that Science will be edified by the information I am about to give you. At the same time, the police of other countries will undoubtedly be interested in examining this list more closely. Let us begin with the house-breaking in the Villa Rosenhain, the home of Stefanson, the bank president."

"What was the value of the articles stolen?" asked the lawyer, taking up his pen.

"At a low estimate, ten thousand crowns," replied Krag.

The lawyer made note of the amount and then said, "Continue!"

"Then we have the robbery at Bjorneby's the ship-chandler's home—bank-notes amounting to three or four thousand crowns."

"Suppose we say four thousand," murmured the lawyer.

"Then we have the robbery of the money-safe in the apartment of Wold, the retired banker. Twenty thousand crowns!"

The lawyer again noted the amount, but he did so with a sigh.

"Go on," he said.

"Besides that we have the affair in the National Theatre, where five gentlemen in the front row orchestra seats had their pockets picked of more than four thousand crowns. Among them was the king's guest, Prince Chira of Siam who lost, among other things, his Grand Cross of the Order of St. Olav."

"What? And how great a value do you place on it?"

"I should say that in its ordinary form the Grand Cross might be valued at two thousand crowns."

"Was this Cross unusual in any way?"

"Yes, Prince Chira had provided it with a special setting of diamonds. It did not seem splendid enough for him when he received it in Christiania. And for that reason we shall have to value it at thirty thousand crowns."

And Krag went on counting and checking off one robbery after another. It was a long, amazing list. But the lawyer wrote down the sums without a single objection. When the guests who had been robbed at Consul Birger's poker evening were reached, the lawyer bowed his head over his memorandum-book.

The Chief of Police said, severely: "My dear sir, it looks to me as though you were smiling!"

"Not at all," said Chevillard, after a short silence, looking up, "I have seldom been so entirely serious as at the present moment."

And then came the theft of the Chief of Police's own furniture.

"Is that possible?" asked the lawyer. "Do you mean to say that all the furniture of the Chief of Police was stolen from his home?"

"Everything," said the Chief, "everything except my Turkish pepper-box. That was not stolen!"

Again the lawyer's head dropped over his memorandum-book.

The Chief hemmed and hawed and shifted about the papers.

The lawyer looked up. His eyes were moist as though there were tears in them. But then, French lawyers can be moved to tears whenever it seems necessary.

"I regret very much the abominal way in which the Chief of Police himself has been stripped bare. But the fact that my client selected the Chief of Police as one of his victims, speaks in his favor."

"You think so? It seems to me such a piece of impudence makes his case all the worse."

"Quite so, quite so—in a way! But it also shows that my client has acted with a certain chivalry. It shows that he feared no one. And I do not for a moment feel that this little episode should be hushed up. I am quite certain, my dear Chief of Police, that you will not try to suppress or make a secret of this little theft merely because, if it were made public, people could not help but laugh at you."

The Chief of Police cleared his throat vigorously.

"So far as that goes," the lawyer continued, "there is no reason why my client should be shown any consideration. On the other hand, I would suggest that in view of my client's great scientific services, and since his actions were all prompted by an ideal motive, some consideration be shown him. Especially since he is ready to make good all losses and whatever damage he may have caused."

"You speak of the thief's ideal aims," said Asbjörn Krag. "Will you be kind enough to explain this a little more in detail?"

"My client really is a great idealist," replied the lawyer. "He is absolutely unselfish." In that respect he is a unique figure in the history of crime. My client never steals in order to obtain money."

"But you have not yet explained to us why he steals at all. We have been waiting to hear the reason for some time."

"He steals because he has to steal."

"That is no explanation," said the Chief of Police, reproachfully. "The old excuse of kleptomania does not fit in here at all. These thefts and robberies have nothing to do with kleptomania. And, at all events, there is no gang of thieves *all* of whose members are kleptomaniacs."

"Of how many persons does Mr. d'Albert's gang consist?" asked the lawyer.

"There are five or six, at the very least. We caught one of his best men, but he escaped last night from jail."

"Let me explain the whole thing to you," said the lawyer. "You know Mr. d'Albert's wonderful linguistic accomplishments. He speaks Norwegian like a native."

"He even speaks Norwegian with a pronounced Christiania twang," replied Krag. "No one would ever suspect that he is not a Norwegian."

"Quite so. He has astonished other individuals of other nations in the same way. He has studied all dead and living tongues. He has published several authoritative works on ancient Egyptian dialects. He has pointed out and proven the relationship between Asiatic and primal American idioms, and his lectures on the employment of the subjunctive clause in the Aztec sentence made a sensation in Paris, and assured him a place among the most eminent philologists. In your investigations, gentlemen, you no doubt have discovered various notes written by my client, notes whose meaning was hard to decipher. Is that not so?"

Krag recalled the mysterious sentences which he had found scribbled on the sheets of note-paper in d'Albert's room at the Victoria Hotel.

"I do recall some mysterious sentences of the kind," he replied.

"Might I ask what they were?"

Krag took out his note-book and read: "Bamboo grows in the shade."

"It sounds like something, gentlemen, but what does it mean?"

"At first glance it seems quite devoid of meaning. A literal French translation would be as follows: *La canne croit dans l'ombre*. But that does not make it any the more sensible."

When the lawyer heard the French translation he cried out joyfully: "I understand! I understand! That makes me the happiest man on earth!"

The two Norwegians looked at him in surprise, and once more something in their eyes seemed to hint that they were beginning to doubt the stranger's honesty of purpose. It was true that he had his papers, and everything pointed to his being the person whom he represented himself to be, but still . . ."

"*La canne croit dans l'ombre,*" repeated the Frenchman, seemingly delighted. "That is excellent. Then all my suppositions have been proven correct. Do you know what those words mean, gentlemen?"

"In Norwegian," Krag replied, "or rather, in our local thieves' slang, the sentence means that danger threatens."

"That agrees perfectly with the French meaning. But what danger is meant, do you think?"

"It is not a danger which would threaten either of us. I have heard pickpockets and other criminals use the expression when they noticed that they were in danger, that is when the police were on their tracks. 'Bamboo' is a Christiania slang name for a policeman. So 'Bamboo is growing in the shade,' means 'The police are close at hand, they are watching.' It is a warning."

"The expression has exactly the same meaning in the thieves' *argot* of Paris, as you probably know," replied the lawyer.

"Did the remarkable man leave any other notice of the same kind lying around?"

Then Krag read aloud the two other sentences he had found on d'Albert's writing-desk. They had similar meanings. Krag translated them into French and told what they meant in the lingo of the underworld. To the lawyer's lively joy, it turned out that the expressions had related forms in the Parisian criminal *argot*.

"And surely now you are willing to admit," said the lawyer, "that we have made a step in advance toward the solution of the riddle."

"Yes," replied Krag. "I am quite ready to admit it. Mr. d'Albert's intimate acquaintance with the slang of the underworld points to the most natural solution of the riddle in the world, in view of what has taken place. It seems to prove that the gentleman in question is one of the most daring and skilful criminals who ever operated in Christiania."

"Not at all," replied the lawyer, "on the contrary, the circumstance is a link in my chain of evidence, which proves the direct opposite!"

"How do you make out any such thing?" asked the Chief of Police. "And do you mind telling me, my dear sir, how you yourself happen to have such an extensive knowledge of the thieves' jargon. You must admit that it is something decidedly unusual."

Again the lawyer's face grew serious.

"The connection is quite near at hand," he replied. "In order to help my client out of the numerous difficulties in which he entangles himself I have been compelled to follow him through thick and thin. I have had to sound the hidden depths of his life, his manner of work, his mode of thought. And thus I have gained a wide acquaintance with these things. Nor should you forget that my activities as a lawyer of the French criminal courts has been an excellent preparatory school for a correct understanding of the secret and hidden meanings of the underworld tongue."

"Very well! In that case you merely owe us an explanation as to why your client who, according to your own statement, is a distinguished scholar, hit upon the idea of appearing in Christiania as a criminal."

"I will not hide the true reason from you," replied the lawyer. "But in order to make everything perfectly clear to you, I shall have to go back somewhat into the past, and review my client's earlier activities as a scholar. From the year 1897 to the year 1901, Mr. d'Albert was in Southern China, in the province of Puh-Fuh."

The Chief of Police and Krag looked at one another. Both quite evidently thought this introduction rather farfetched.

"My client," the lawyer went on, quite unmoved,

"was engrossed at the time in his study of the dialects of Southern China. During the four years of his stay in Puh-Fuh, nothing at all was heard of him in France. For a time it was even thought that he had died. But then came reports from missionaries, and these reports were most surprising. It turned out, in fact, that for a long time d'Albert had been living as a Chinaman. Not among the mandarins of high-caste Chinese, but among the people, among the coolies, the scum of the cities! And—he lived exactly as they did. He dwelt in one of their wretched huts. He ate their food. And in the end he was able, owing to his unique talent, his linguistic gift, to speak their various dialects. It is one of my client's peculiarities that when he studies anything, he studies it from the ground up. And he claims that one can only learn another people's language by living with and among them, and becoming one of them. As I know Mr. d'Albert I do not for a moment doubt that during those years he felt himself a genuine coolie. He dropped his correspondence, his newspapers, his European manners, customs, and clothing. He worked, acted and thought as a coolie. The only difference between him and his fellow-coolies lay in his scholarship. Every evening he noted down his lingual observations in his mss. folios. He might still be living as a coolie in China, quite forgotten, had not Science once more lured him away.   Just as the taciturn naturalist goes from plant to plant in the primeval jungles of the wilderness, so d'Albert went from word to word and from dialect to dialect in the tangled confusion of South-Chinese speech-forms. Finally he began tracing individual words from tribe to tribe.   And in this manner he took the same road which some prehistoric tribal migration might have taken.   He passed out beyond the borders of China and suddenly found himself in India.   And among some tribes south of the Himalayas he once more found the origins of the language he was tracing. He had followed the river on which they dwelt, and has ascended it to its source.   There he halted and looked around.   He had completed his task.   So he shot up like a diver from the depths of his sea of study, and began to ask for the news of Europe, to demand newspapers.   He once more went back to his faultless European clothes, and in the Hotel Imperial at Delhi he wrote his epoch-making work on the dialects of Southern China."

The lawyer had talked himself into a most enthusiastic frame of mind, and at this point drew from his brief-case a thick volume which he showed his two listeners.

On its back the volume bore the following label: "Treatise on the Dialects of Southern China (Researches made in the Province of Puh-Fuh)."

The Chief of Police looked questioningly at Krag.
"I begin to see," said the latter, softly.

"A prize work!" cried the lawyer, waving the
book in his hand. "Crowned by the French Acad-
emy, gentlemen! An epoch-making work, a really
remarkable work!"

"Go on," said Krag, "we are still quite a ways
from the robbery in the Villa Rosenhain."

"Quite true, gentlemen! We are just as far removed from it as Delhi is from Christiania. But
my account of my client's adventures will bring us
nearer to your city. From India he slowly wandered over Afghanistan to Asia Minor, and thence
on to the Caucausus. Here he met with lingual
forms of speech which, so it seemed to him, lacked
all connection with any of the languages he already
knew. Not until he had penetrated far into Hungary
did he discover a few similar and related words.
He found that they were used by a tribe of vaga-
bond gypsies. That was a new turning-point in M.
d'Albert's existence. With the greatest enthusiasm
he flung himself into the study of this mysterious
tongue. And true to his established habit of work,
he did not content himself with studying it super-
ficially. Not at all. He became a gypsy or Tatar
or whatever you choose to call it. For two long
years he wandered through Hungary and Austria
with a band of gypsies. And then, aboard a gypsy

vessel which traded along the Marne, he made his way to the interior of France. He travelled through England with a family of gypsy jugglers. He also lived in a gypsy tent in Scandinavia. His volume covering this mysterious tongue has not as yet appeared. But I think it probable that when it does, it will lift the veil which for centuries has rested on this language and its origins."

"Nor need you think that this has no connection with the matter which concerns us at the moment. Quite the contrary is the case. Disregarding only a few unimportant incidents, I have traced my client's life experiences in a direct line from their beginnings to Christiania. I wish to call special attention to the fact that in his research work he is like no other scholar known to me. What separates him from all others is the unique way in which he identifies himself with the subject-matter of his studies. He is interested not alone in philology itself, he is equally interested in all that surrounds a language, the racial soil from which it has sprung, the life which the language itself radiates. Once he has made up his mind to investigate a language, he first tries to make clear to himself why the language is as it is, and not otherwise. He feels he must *live the same life* which conditioned the development of the language in question. This is what I have tried to make plain to you, gentlemen! I hope I have been able to make myself clear?"

"Nothing could be clearer," replied Krag. "And now all I am waiting for is to hear what you have to say about Christiania."

"Very well. M. d'Albert already had his trip to Christiania in mind while he was busy with his investigation of the mysterious gypsy tongue. As you can easily imagine, gentlemen, this language, in various shadings and dialects, is spread over all Europe. It is spoken by the restless Tatar and by the Tzigane bands which wander from the North to the South of Spain. It differs in different tribes, yet it has a common root. While d'Albert was living among the Tatar tribes, he was struck by the fact that some strange individual words and phrases had been introduced into the language, half jargon, half-word-combinations unclear in meaning, whose origin he could not determine. At least at first he could not do so. But eventually he realized that this strange additional language vocabulary, dealing in part with those activities of the gypsies which shunned the light of day, went back to distant centuries.

"It cannot be denied that the gypsies and the wandering folk have played a very prominent part in the criminal history of the nations. Out of their own individual lives in prison and penitentiaries, out of their constant persecution by the police and the courts, and out of their association with criminals of other races, their language has absorbed a number of expressions which belong to the world of crime. This phase of the idiom aroused d'Albert's attention and fascinated him. And from that moment on he flung himself with the most tremendous enthusiasm into the study of how the language of crime had developed. He found traces of it wherever he went. He recognized the self-same words and expressions. And where a phrase was expressed in different tongues the choice of word-pictures, at any rate, was invariably the same. Like some great linguist who investigates languages long since dead and forgotten, and by reconstructing them obtains a mental picture of the community which spoke them, so my client hit upon a scientifically valid even though fantastic plan. He determined to embody the results of his investigation of crime's international language in a great work, to be entitled: The Migrations of Crime.

"And that is the idea behind this whole mysterious affair. While my client flung himself into the study of the language of crime, he at the same time became a whole-hearted member of the criminal world. It began when he secured admission to certain French government prisons. He did not content himself with visiting them, however. Not at all. He had himself incarcerated as a criminal, and by

listening to the knocking on cell walls and the signals used in prison work-shops, he gathered much
interesting lingual data. He had police officials take
him through the criminal quarters of Paris, and
visited all the most infamous dives and yeggman's
hang-outs. But these surface studies did not especially interest him. He wanted to *live* the actual
life of the criminal and so, one day, he suddenly disappeared. He soon made friends in the sinister,
mysterious world of crime, at first by means of
money, and then owing to his great and uique cleverness and knowledge. Of course, there is a touch
of madness in this manner of scientific study, but I
still claim that M. d'Albert's aims and objectives
have been altogether ideal.

"Take an ordinary burglary, for instance. He
was interested in establishing the concept, the actual
idea of execution of the robbery in all its individual
phases. He wanted to know what lingually important phrases and expressions it might call forth.
And in planning the burglary in question he wished
to learn all the *secret words* and *terms* whispered
over the table in a thieves' hang-out. Then, when
the burglary was carried out, he heard the warning
calls used by the outside men to announce the ap-
proach of danger, or the expressions indicating that
all was well. I can assure you, gentlemen, that in
order to add to his lingual knowledge, to discover

all these idiomatic terms, he was quite capable of staging a burglary! And in this way he has lived the language of crime in one country after another. The madness of his system, naturally, became increasingly apparent, yet it is certain that not for a moment did it occur to him that he was doing anything wrong or infamous. It was merely that his craze for scientific knowledge had blinded him. And yet I would put my hand in the fire this minute to testify that in spite of his manner of life he has remained quite pure and uncontaminated in soul.

"His method suggests that of the vivisectionist who, in order to attain some scientific result for which he is striving, does not hesitate to inflict the greatest suffering on his fellow-creatures. In M. d'Albert's case, it should be added, he himself and the institutions he created, have been exploited in the most incredible way by the criminal elements with whom he surrounded himself. In his strange travels he at last reached your country, gentlemen, and here his insanity—if you wish to use the word— reached its climax. Yet the very circumstance that he sent for me proves that he has completed his investigations, and is once more about to emerge into the light of publicity. Such, gentlemen, is the real explanation of M. d'Albert's crimes, and of how it is possible to be a scholar, a multimillionaire, and a thief at one and the same time!"

EPILOGUE

This is the end of the tale of the man who plundered Christiania. After many conferences and discussions on the part of the police authorities, the state department of justice, the French ambassador, and the Norwegian government, it was decided not to prosecute d'Albert. This result was mainly due to d'Albert's voluntary offer—he was surprised by Krag shortly after his lawyer's explanation, engaged in a profound scientific discussion with Dr. Salinger in Theater Street—to live under observation in an insane asylum for the period of one year. Besides, the fact that he had sent his "gangsters" to Spain where, with his aid, they could once more become useful members of society, weighed in his favor. The red-haired waiter and Thollon also went abroad as soon as they were released from jail.

Incidentally, all the victims of d'Albert's robberies were generously reimbursed, and, in addition, d'Albert paid into the Norwegian state treasury a sum which amounted to one-third his entire fortune. In the insane asylum d'Albert devoted his entire time to writing his great work, and at the end of the year left Norway, never again to play a part in the dark world of crime.